GODDESS GAMES

GODDESS GAMES

GAMES

NIKI BURNHAM

Simon & Schuster Books for Young Readers
New York London Toronto Sydney

SIMON & SCHUSTER BOOKS FOR YOUNG READERS

An imprint of Simon & Schuster Children's Publishing Division

1230 Avenue of the Americas, New York, New York 10020

SIMON & SCHUSTER BOOKS FOR YOUNG READERS is a trademark of Simon & Schuster, Inc.

Book design by Jessica Sonkin

The text for this book is set in Filosofia.

Manufactured in the United States of America

10 9 8 7 6 5 4 3 2 1

Library of Congress Cataloging-in-Publication Data

Burnham, Niki, 1970–

Goddess games / Niki Burnham.—1st ed.

p. cm.

Summary: Three high-school girls from very different social backgrounds deal with their problems and learn how to get along together while working at a mountain resort for the summer.

ISBN-13: 978-1-4169-2700-6 (hardcover)

ISBN-10: 1-4169-2700-X (hardcover)

[1. Resorts—Fiction. 2. Interpersonal relations—Fiction. 3. Colorado—Fiction.] I. Title.

PZ7.B9352Go 2007

[Fic]—dc22

2006031893

FOR MY PARENTS,
WHO GAVE THIRTY-PLUS YEARS
TO THE MILITARY AND AN
ADVENTUROUS CHILDHOOD TO
ME.

✻✻✻

ACKNOWLEDGMENTS

This book was loved and cared for by Julia Richardson, Siobhan Wallace, Jess Sonkin, and Paul Crichton at Simon & Schuster. Special thanks also go to my agent, Steve Axelrod, and to Lori Antonson, who always have my back. I feel fortunate to work with such talented people.

*** one ***

"Excuse me, miss? You working here for the summer?"

The voice coming from behind Claire Watts had a shriek factor measurable on the Richter scale. She spun around to see a forty-something woman lumbering across the asphalt. Even from six parking spots away, Claire immediately spotted a mole with the mass and topography of Mount Evans protruding from the shrieker's cheek.

"Yes, I am." With graciousness she'd perfected working retail for her dad, Claire added, "How did you know?"

Wouldn't a normal person see a plastic surgeon about getting a mole like that removed? Not because it was aesthetically revolting—not really—but because every *Allure* article she'd ever read warned that irregular moles like that were just cancer waiting to sprout.

"You can't park here. Guests only." The woman stopped an arm's length from Claire, huffed out a cinnamon-laced breath, and pointed away from the parking lot, toward a small drive that wound around the back of the King's Crown Resort and Spa. "Employee lot is 'round that way. You may unload your belongings there after you pick up the key to your assigned cabin at the employee registration desk. Doesn't open for another hour, though."

The woman had pain in the ass—correction, pain in the *neck*—written all over her, but Claire kept her smile in place and gestured toward the empty backseat of her six-year-old black Lexus, a hand-me-down after her mother purchased a hybrid luxury sedan in an attempt to be earth-friendly. "I'm not actually unloading anything today. I'm local, so I'm waiting until tomorrow morning to check in. But I was driving by and thought I would stop in to make sure I'm not missing any paperwork or anything."

Run-ins with know-it-alls like this woman were just God's way of testing her. Claire was determined to meet the challenge instead of firing off the kind of sarcastic reply she would have used a few short months ago. Besides, wasn't that what this summer was supposed to be about? Getting her head together and getting things right with God? Practicing being a good Christian, so when school started again in the fall the behavior would be habit instead of such a struggle?

Maybe then the kids at Teen Jam would take her seriously. Not that it really mattered if they ever did—her rediscovery of Christianity was between her and God—but it'd sure make life easier. And she really wanted to go on the Mexico trip they were planning over Thanksgiving, to help rebuild a school that had been wiped out in a hurricane. She hadn't worked up the guts to volunteer yet—it'd mean convincing her parents and volunteering a lot of time on fund-raising projects to help pay for everything—but how great would it be to help kids like that?

"You'll still need to go around to the back. No employee vehicles are permitted in the guest lot."

"No problem. Sorry." Claire tried to look deferential and professional at the same time, though it was hard to achieve in flip-flops, cropped khaki pants, and a basic white Calvin Klein tee. No matter how casual her clothing, it bugged Claire that the woman was treating her this way. How many times had the Watts family come here for Sunday brunch? Recommended it to out-of-towners looking for a luxe place to stay?

But whatever.

Claire pulled her keys back out of her purse, then shot a pointed look at the older woman's silver name tag, neatly pinned opposite the embroidered King's Crown logo on her hunter green polo shirt. "You're Marla, I take it? It's nice to meet you." She stepped forward and extended a hand. "I'm Claire Watts. I understand I'm to be assigned to the information desk. I'm sure we'll be seeing—"

"Orientation starts promptly at nine tomorrow morning, so you'll need to get here early and park in the back." Hands on her size twenty-four (if Claire had to guess) hips, she added, "And no dilly-dallying at a coffee shop or any of that other stuff you teenagers like to do in the mornings. We have a lot of ground to cover and we'll be starting right on time."

Claire pulled her hand back as Marla eyed the small dent in the side of Claire's vehicle—parked at the end of a long row of pristine BMWs, Jaguars, and Mercedes all spaced just so in the hope that no one would suffer door dings—and made a face.

Whatta bitch!

Claire instantly gave herself a mental smackdown. Even if she didn't *say* the b-word, wasn't thinking it just as bad in God's eyes? Training herself not to *think* bad words was more difficult than she'd expected, but with work she'd get there.

And then she could work on the rest of her thoughts.

She shouldn't think less of Marla for her weight. For her mole. For anything. It was just *wrong*.

"All right. Thank you so much, Marla."

She slid into the front seat of her Lexus, then backed up carefully—despite the temptation to hit the gas hard enough to make Marla worry about her toes getting crushed—and turned toward the narrow road leading to the employee cabins.

This is God's plan for me. She repeated it twice more, out loud, just to help the fact sink into her brain.

God wouldn't have steered her toward a job at the information desk at King's Crown—and away from working another summer at one of Dad's high-end sporting goods stores, hawking mountain bikes and hiking equipment to wealthy vacationers—if He didn't mean for it to enrich her life in some way. Just like He wouldn't have had her sitting on the bench in Ritter Park the day after the worst day of her life. She'd been picking at the peeling green paint, wondering where she'd gone wrong and how she could fix her life, when her ears caught the conversation of a group of kids sitting near the rocks behind her. They'd started talking about Teen Jam, and the sense of belonging and happiness they'd exuded piqued her curiosity. Then they'd talked about the Mexico trip and the opportunity to help kids in need.

It was like He'd popped her in the middle of her forehead and shouted, "Here is what you must do!"

She put the Lexus in park, turned off the ignition, then leaned back in the seat, taking a few moments to study the rows of 1970s-era log cabins nestled amongst the trees at the lowest point on the King's Crown property so they were out of the direct line of sight of the guest rooms. Starting tomorrow, one of those cabins would be her home.

It was a world away from her parents' sprawling post-and-beam home on the other side of town, with its ultra-contemporary furnishings, gorgeous modern art, and rows of floor-to-ceiling windows positioned for maximum views of the evergreen-blanketed mountains. And with two roommates, it'd be cramped.

She couldn't wait.

Thank God—and she really did thank God—her parents agreed to allow her to stay here with the rest of the summer employees instead of commuting from home. For the next three months she'd be free of her parents' constant nagging about her "personality swings" and questions about whether she was "experimenting with drugs."

Ha. If she told them what was really up, they'd croak.

Not that it was really an option to have a heart-to-heart with them. If they were gut-level honest with themselves, her parents didn't really want to know what was up with their only daughter. As great as her parents might be, Claire knew their questions about her recent goody-goody behavior—and the weeks of grumpy silence, stomach upset, and tears that preceded her turnaround—didn't come because they were concerned for her well-being and wanted a TV sitcom–style parental chat in hopes of making it all better.

Claire was certain they *believed* they cared about her, but in truth they just wanted to make sure she wasn't doing anything that could hurt the family's reputation—and Summit SuperSport—if she got caught at whatever it was they suspected her of doing.

If she acted happy and made the occasional comment about how much she liked her job, by the time school started again in the fall their questions would dissipate.

Poof.

Mom and Dad would start talking in their bedroom one night (once they thought Claire was asleep) about how she must've gone through a rough patch during the spring—maybe they'd use the word *phase*—but thankfully everything turned out all right. They might even congratulate themselves on the fact they let Claire solve her mysterious mini-crisis herself.

Idiots. She loved them, but they were clueless about her personal life.

Claire touched up her lip gloss, fluffed her newly highlighted hair, then headed up the path from the employee parking lot to the main lodge. The whole place was quiet, with the exception of the gurgling mountain creek that ran past the spa building, adding to the ambience for those who chose to have outdoor massages. Just the right kind of setting for her to engage in reflection, study her Bible, and figure out what it was God wanted her to do now. How she should go forward with her life from here and who that life should include.

If it should include Aaron.

She wanted him so bad it physically hurt.

She yanked open the back door of the main lodge harder than necessary, wishing her life hadn't come to this but knowing it had been her own fault. And knowing that things would be much, much worse at this moment if God hadn't given her a second chance, though she felt pretty guilty about the method by which she'd been given that second chance.

God, please just let Aaron love me like he always has. Give me that much?

His plane landed in less than twenty-four hours. She figured in about forty-eight she'd know God's plan where Aaron was concerned.

As she stood at the front desk waiting for someone to direct her to the office of the summer hire coordinator, she wondered: Does God consider it a sin to pray that the guy you've been fornicating with won't dump you?

✽✽✽ TWO ✽✽✽

The last sixteen hours constituted the worst kind of hell for Drew Davenport. No air-conditioning, no place to stretch her legs, and the constant smell of other people's body odor in her nostrils made her cranky as hell.

She needed to run. Bad.

Drew sucked the last bit of her Edensoy vanilla soy milk through the straw, then flipped the box into the trash receptacle near the front door of the King's Crown Resort and Spa while she waited for the driver to unload her bag from the underbelly of the bus. He grunted as he reached for the oversize black Adidas duffel bag Drew's mom had gotten for her at the Leavenworth PX—of course he'd handed out the Louis Vuitton and Gucci bags to their owners first—then dropped it onto the sidewalk next to her as if it contained dumbbells. Which it did, but still. What a wuss.

It was cool and breezy up here in the mountains,

unlike the unseasonably warm ninety-seven degrees she'd left behind in Kansas the day before. After being crammed in a narrow bus seat next to a woman who snored the entire way to Denver, waiting at the downtown bus station for her transfer to Juniper, then trying not to yak up her guts as the bus teetered around corners during the climb into the mountains, she'd had it. Her sixteen-hour trip from hell gave her the right to grunt aloud, unlike the bus driver, who'd spent the last two hours in a cushy seat with armrests and access to the air-conditioning controls.

Drew pulled her money stash out of the front pocket of her shorts, then carefully unrolled not one, but two bills for the driver. She shot him an appreciative smile as she pressed the money into his hand. He might be completely lazy, but he did drive a high-class resort bus, the kind with luxury seating and a real bathroom, not a crappy, please-don't-get-a-flat bus like the one she'd taken from Leavenworth to Denver. She supposed he deserved two bucks for a tip instead of one, just due to the class factor.

He didn't look thankful, though, which only succeeded in darkening Drew's mood.

The driver started to climb back into the bus, but hesitated and looked over his shoulder at Drew. She didn't miss his perusal of her legs—everyone stared at her legs, especially when they were tan, like they were now from track season, so she was used to it—but something else in his eyes made her want to smack him.

"You got a problem or something?" She asked when she realized he wasn't going to simply sit down, close the doors, and drive away.

"Just wondering if you needed directions or help getting somewhere, ma'am," he replied. He turned on the steps to face her, though his gaze remained fixed lower, on her legs. "Maybe you'd like some dinner recommendations in town? I know all the best places."

"I'm fine. I'm working here for the summer so I'm eating the employee meals."

"Oh." He finally met her eyes, and she could see the wheels in his mind spinning: *Damn . . . the girl's just trash. Nothing worth pursuing here.*

She hefted her duffel over her shoulder—making it clear that the effort wasn't what he'd made it out to be while unloading it—and mentally told him off with a *Whatever, 'cause you wouldn't have a shot with me anyway, you perv.*

He returned to his seat, his weight triggering a loud cushion fart. Drew gave him a look that let him know she'd heard, then turned away before he could close the doors on her.

The regular hotel guests followed the bellmen indoors to check into their weeklong escape from reality, but Drew took her time, discreetly stretching her hamstrings with a forward bend—once the bus driver took off and she could be sure he wasn't checking out her rear—before strolling into the lobby. Her first look around took her breath away. You'd never find a resort built entirely of logs—complete with a monstrous stone fireplace, a painting of a Rocky Mountain sunset, and several expensive-looking Mexican rugs—anywhere near Leavenworth, and yippee for that. She needed something different.

She needed to call Aunt Jo in Colorado Springs and thank her for forwarding the link to the King's Crown website, complete with suggestions for filling out the summer job application.

Only three weeks ago she thought she'd be spending this summer just like last summer, shuffling pizzas through the conveyor belt–style oven at her next-door neighbor's pizza joint. She'd get home after midnight in her rancid clothes, then strip in the back hall so she could toss them in the washer immediately to keep her bedroom from reeking of stale tomato sauce and garlic bread. She'd crawl under the covers, exhausted, forced to listen to her mom's television through the thin walls of their new house, knowing Mom would only stir from her bed long enough to go to work at the library, mope for eight hours there, then come back home to mope some more in front of Letterman.

On a good day Mom might get some laundry done. On a really good day there'd be food in the house. But most days, Drew had to scrounge. Getting Mom to the grocery store was more work than it was worth. Better for Drew to steal a twenty from Mom's wallet and hit the store herself for some cans of soup, apples, bread, and organic peanut butter.

Nothing her new roommates might do could be more tortuous than moving between what she'd come to think of as the Two Circles of Hell—one at home with Mom, the other at school (the School Circle being replaced by the Pizza Palace Circle during the summer).

Plus, not only would she be able to make more money here—*way* more—she'd be able to train at high altitude, the way a world-class runner would. She could breathe in the scent of pine needles while her feet pounded along trail after trail, then come fall she'd totally rock at cross-country. She broke the school record two months ago in the 2,000 meters and was only eight seconds off the state record. What more could she accomplish after a summer training here? Win the state championship in cross-country? Obliterate the state record in the 2,000 during track season? The gently rolling hills where Leavenworth sat above the Missouri River would be nothing after mastering this terrain.

Eight seconds would be *nothing*.

She could picture her name up on the wall of the Leavenworth High School gymnasium right now, on the banner they presented to your school when you broke a state record. Even if someone else eventually broke her record, the banner would be there forever.

With any luck one of her roommates would be a runner, too. The information packet they'd sent her when she'd received the job offer said she'd be staying in one of the employee cabins with a girl from Los Angeles named Seneca Billeray (which kind of sounded familiar, though why, she couldn't say), and *Shape* magazine was always talking about how people in L.A. liked to go running on the beach and hiking in the hills. The other roommate sounded even more promising—a local girl named Claire Watts. Surely someone who lived around here would be the outdoorsy type and up for some trail running. And Claire would already be used to the altitude, so keeping up with her would be a good challenge.

The sooner she met them, the better. Her body needed to *move*. And then it was going to need lunch—something healthier than the glazed doughnut she'd grabbed for breakfast at the Denver bus terminal.

By the time she'd checked in at the desk bearing a handwritten NEW EMPLOYEES sign and picked up her paperwork, the duffel bag was starting to dig into her shoulder and she was beginning to wish she'd just told off the pervy bus driver. It would've made her feel better.

However, the instant she went out the main lodge's back door and her feet hit the dirt trail leading to the employee cabins, huddled in a group of evergreens about two hundred yards away, the bag felt weightless and she could have cared less about the asshole who drove the bus.

Wow, but this had been the right decision. How cool was it going to be to lead hikes through this area all summer long? She walked toward the cabins, pausing at a large map of the resort grounds so she could take a couple minutes to study the trails, noting which ones were marked easy, moderate, advanced, and strenuous. Maybe tonight she'd start easy, just to get used to the altitude. But by summer's end she was going to cruise on the Aspen Leaf trail, a hilly six-mile route labeled in red as Strenuous. If she could conquer that one . . .

"You need help?"

Drew turned to see a guy about her own age—maybe a year older—walking up behind her, apparently coming from the lodge.

He was so not Leavenworth. This guy made her mouth water. Actually *water*. Or maybe that was just the fact she hadn't eaten in a few hours and she'd spun around too fast.

"I'm fine. Just studying the trails," she replied, hoping she didn't sound like a total doorknob.

"If you have any questions, ask me." He grinned. "My name's Rob. Rob Lucherini. I'm one of the trail guides. Well, I will be, starting tomorrow."

"Hey, me too." She stuck out a hand. Even though she always felt weird doing it, her parents had drilled it into her when she was little. "I'm Drew Davenport."

Rob had a firm grip, but not firm like some guys, who'd try to show Drew how tough they were by giving her a handshake meant to break every one of her fingers. There was the lightest dusting of dark hair on the back of his hand. Enough to be masculine, but not so much Drew automatically suspected the guy had a hairy back.

Her mouth watered all over again. The guy had to be six-two, with a lean, tight build that made him look like he could run the Aspen Leaf trail without getting winded.

"Thought so," he said, then let go of her hand to point to the orientation packet tucked under her arm. "All the forms are a pain to fill out, but we have until tomorrow morning to get it done. You see your cabin yet?"

"No. Are they that bad?"

One side of his mouth ratcheted up. Totally sexy, but in a way that let Drew know he found her pretty hot, too. Good. She never, ever wanted to be attracted to a guy who wasn't just as attracted to her—and more. Girls who chased after guys made her want to heave. It was like they thought guys were better than they were, just for being born with a Y chromosome, and that it would be the ultimate in life just to spend time with someone blessed by a freak pre-birth occurrence. Please.

"Nah. Not exactly roomy, though. You better hope you like your roommates."

"I'm sure I'll be fine." Drew shot him a confident grin, then made a show of shifting her duffel bag on her shoulder. "I should probably go dump my stuff. Nice to meet you though, Rob."

The slight drop in his shoulders gave her a momentary power rush. "Ditto."

"See you tomorrow at orientation."

"Actually, I get to skip it. I worked here last summer." He bent down to tighten the lace on one shoe. The latest trail runners, Drew noticed. "But all the guides do a hike together tomorrow morning after orientation. Sort of a here's-how-you're-going-to-do-it demonstration. So I'll see you then."

"See you then." Oh, definitely. Maybe he'd be a good running partner, too.

She took the trail down a slight hill toward her cabin. Maybe she'd try out one of the moderate trails right away, now that her usual self-assurance had come back, replacing the annoyance her bus trip had caused. She sucked in the fresh morning air, which only served to stoke her enthusiasm.

Oh, yeah. Today she could fly, even without her fave rap tunes blasting from her iPod, driving her harder and faster. She opened the screen door to cabin number nine, held it behind her with her rear, then slid her key into the lock on the thick pine door.

It was nearly ten A.M., but she could barely make out the cabin's interior. A flight of stairs was immediately to her left, apparently leading to the sleeping area. A television stood on a black melamine cabinet in the corner opposite her, with a couch facing it. Between the couch and the television, two rustic armchairs sided a dark-stained pine coffee table. The whole place smelled like it had been the scene of many, many drinking games. Maybe she'd open the windows before going on her run. Air the place out a little.

She dropped her duffel bag on the floor at the base of the stairs, then located the nearest light switch and flipped it on so she wouldn't break her neck going up.

Something moved on the couch, then a pillow came flying toward her head, just missing her before landing at the foot of the stairs. "Whoever you are, shut the door and turn that damned light off already! People are trying to sleep."

People?

"Um, I'm Drew. I live here," Drew said.

"Yeah? Goody for you, 'cause so do I. And I'm *sleeping*. Kill the light."

Drew flicked off the light, then fumbled her way upstairs and turned on the light up there. If "people" had a problem with that light being on, then screw them.

She should have left the one downstairs on.

"Geez." Drew looked around the room before setting her duffel on one of the two empty beds. The thing that moved on the sofa was apparently her roommate, and judging from the fact that one bed and more than half the floor space were filled with the girl's stuff—which included several pairs of designer sunglasses, fancy shoes, and a pristine Louis Vuitton suitcase—even though three people were supposed to be sleeping in this one room, Drew figured this had to be the L.A. roomie.

How peachy keen and swell. She was going to be spending the summer with an overblown stereotype of a Hollywood rich kid. One who slept in the middle of the day, too.

As she left for her run five minutes later, Drew accidentally and on purpose nudged one of the downstairs window shades so light spilled across the room in a line leading directly to the couch. Then she pulled the door shut behind her—hard.

✻✻✻ THREE ✻✻✻

The Beatles were inside Seneca Billeray's head. Not only because she was buzzed on Grey Goose and tonic and imagining a grizzly Ringo Starr pounding on a drum set inside her skull (though someone mentioned that the girl wearing the slinky tangerine halter and flirting with the bartender an hour or so ago was Ringo's stepdaughter. She needed to find a computer and search online later to see if he even had one). It was more the Beatles' words.

Get back, get back. Get back to where you once belonged.

And this was where she belonged. Sitting on the patio at The Final Run, with a gentle mountain breeze blowing through her meticulously styled black hair and a guy she'd never met trying to balance a shot glass on her ankle. Partying with the sons and daughters of other important people, just as she had partied with them a year ago, before her mother broke up with her big-shot producer boyfriend, Axel Randolph, and they were forced to cut short their summer vacation at his six-bedroom, five-bath home just outside Juniper. The house with the indoor waterfall and a wood-paneled home theater, complete with its own popcorn machine.

She most certainly did *not* belong in Culver-freaking-City, California, comparing the asking prices on three-bedroom houses now that her mother thought they should sell their spacious home in Beverly Hills. Really, didn't the woman have any sense? Seneca knew if she and her mom moved there, it was all over. No Academy Award–winning actress—at least, not one who deserved her golden statuette—would live in a so-called "modest home" in Culver City. Directors and casting agents would smell the desperation on Jacqueline Billeray the moment she walked in for an audition.

Wasn't it insult enough Mom had to *audition*?

And if her mother fell off the A-list—well, it was probably the B-plus- or maybe even the plain B-list now—then Seneca would have a damned hard time getting into clubs, finagling designer discounts, and staying on the invite list for all the best parties. No one wanted to associate with someone who didn't have the potential to become the Next Big Thing.

Ever since the day they'd flown home from Axel's house and Mom sat her down to tell her that if another big movie role didn't come along soon Seneca might be tossing her favorite Vivienne Tam dress and coordinating Pierre Hardy shoes into a pile destined for a resale shop, Seneca had sworn she'd do whatever it took to keep their heads above water. And she'd do it with style.

She'd make sure her mother landed another Oscar-worthy role. One that would show off Jacqueline's talents (because the woman was amazingly talented) and make her a lock for future work so they'd never have to worry about kissing up to arrogant jackasses like Axel Randolph again. Well, and so they could both use their platinum cards without worrying about how to pay the bills.

Seneca had suffered enough already. It was bad enough seeing the maid go. Mom had employed Melanie since before Seneca was born and, though the woman was odd, she was honest and actually got their house clean. But Melanie was far too expensive now, with Mom only getting the occasional guest spot on made-for-TV dramas and catch-as-catch-can voiceover work, rather than the big-money roles she'd gotten throughout the eighties and nineties. Especially without Axel footing the bills, insisting that he'd rather pay Melanie's salary himself than see Mom take a movie that would have her away on a shoot for three or four months at a crack.

For Seneca, what had been almost as bad as losing Melanie was watching her Mercedes coupe back down the driveway with its new owner at the wheel. Giving up her sweet sixteen gift was excruciating but necessary, Mom explained, since it was just a back-and-forth-to-school car and Seneca could always bum rides with friends while claiming to be shopping for new wheels.

But now that Mom had forced her to get a summer job and was talking the distinct possibility of *Culver City* if things didn't turn around . . . how much worse could it get?

It was destiny Seneca saw the ad for the King's Crown Resort and Spa's yoga studio. Everyone who was anyone stayed at King's Crown, and if she could mix and mingle with the right people this summer, maybe she could snag her mom some auditions—auditions Mom's agent suddenly seemed unwilling or unable to get for his famous client.

Axel's doing, Jacqueline suspected, but her agent had a lot of clout and Jacqueline wasn't ready to cut him loose quite yet. Not until she knew for certain he'd succumbed to pressure from Axel. And not until she had another (good) agent lined up and willing to bust his hump for her.

The shot glass fell off Seneca's ankle and bounced along the flagstones.

"Oops," Mystery Guy mumbled. He watched the shot glass roll in a slow circle, then come to rest against the leg of his chair. Unable or unwilling to reach for it, he fell back against the cushions, Seneca's ankle still cradled in his lap. Seneca didn't mind. Well, not really. The guy was terribly hot. But without the shot glass there serving a specific purpose, having her ankle in his lap just made her look like a slut. And Seneca was *not* a slut.

In fact, she was probably the only person in the whole bar who was still a virgin.

"You know, you're a beautiful girl, Stephanie." Mystery Guy's blue eyes were glassy beneath his perfectly combed black hair, but his speech was clear enough for Seneca to know he'd be alert a while longer.

Not that she wanted him to be. She still didn't know his name, and names were everything in Juniper. No way would she waste a perfectly good night on a loser. If he couldn't move her up the social ladder, he wasn't worth it.

Though if he *was* somebody, she'd make damned certain he got *her* name right.

"It's Seneca, sweetie." She hadn't used that deep, seductive tone in months and was thrilled to discover she could still pull it off. "You tell me who you are and I'll think about letting you keep that ankle."

"Mmm," he murmured, rewarding her with a lazy

grin. His eyes sharpened and Seneca straightened in response, knowing who had to be behind her.

Dahlia Koss glanced at the guy cradling Seneca's strappy Stuart Weitzman sandal in his lap—a style Seneca feared Dahlia would recognize as being several years old—then focused her gaze on Seneca. "We're outta here. You coming? Or staying with this freak?"

"Hey—"

"Shut up, Frankie. Seneca's way too good for you."

Taking the hint, Seneca withdrew her foot. She might have temporarily fallen to the bottom of the social ladder—well, she would if Dahlia and her younger sister, Violet, ever found out Seneca was *working* at King's Crown, not *staying* there—but Frankie what's-his-name was clearly lower than low. At least in Dahlia Koss's eyes, and that's what counted if Seneca wanted to spend her summer cementing her connections around town.

She was lucky Dahlia and Violet even invited her along tonight, given that she hadn't seen them since her mother ditched Axel, and Axel was a good friend of Dahlia and Violet's dad, a record company exec. Damn good thing she'd run into them while she was window-shopping at Kitson in downtown Juniper after her incredibly rude roommate woke her from her hangover-induced nap this morning. It wasn't as good as bumping into some old but still well-connected casting agent who'd "always been a fan!" of her mom's, but it was good enough. Dahlia and Violet invited her to their father's birthday extravaganza at Juniper's most popular hangout, and hence her evening thus far.

Who'd have thought attending a party for someone turning fifty could be so much fun? Probably because it was all arranged by Mr. Koss's new wife, who was in her late twenties or early thirties, tops.

"I'm definitely coming with you." Seneca stood and smoothed her Dolce & Gabbana miniskirt—the one new item she owned, purchased this afternoon with the last of her savings just so Dahlia and Violet wouldn't suspect money was so tight that Seneca's mom could no longer afford to both have her vegan meals delivered and keep up her Botox treatments—then spun away from Frankie as if they'd never spoken.

Apparently it was the right move, since Dahlia smiled, then linked arms with her and guided her toward the door, where Violet was waiting with a lit Marlboro Light casually held between lips tinted with her signature Nars Daredevil gloss.

"Ready to blow?" Violet dangled the keys to her BMW convertible from a freshly manicured fingertip.

Dahlia just grinned, knowing that at least a few of the

males in The Final Run would soon be jumping in their own cars to see where the Koss girls had gone. They'd be on their cell phones, trying to discover if the two blondes had gone to another party—maybe one with some movie people instead of all the music industry people at this party—at Tabby's Bar or at one of the three places Arnold Schwarzenegger owned in town. And that was the way it should be.

She might have to sit in the backseat of the Beemer by herself while Dahlia and Violet took starring roles up front, but she didn't care. Just being with the Koss girls again meant she was back *in*. And once she felt like she was truly back in the social groove, she could ditch them. They were complete airheads, anyway.

Dahlia belched loudly as Violet turned the key in the ignition, which brought giggles from all three. Seneca suddenly wondered if Violet was sober enough to negotiate Juniper's narrow downtown strip or the winding road that led up the mountain to a few of the other popular bars, but dismissed the thought when Violet unscrewed the cap on a bottle of Evian and took a long swig.

Violet never drank water in between her real drinks. She was a purist. All alcohol for a twenty-four-hour period, or all water, depending on how she felt about the bathroom scale on any given day.

Seneca leaned her head back against the leather seat, reveling in the top-down luxury of Violet's car. Damn, but it felt good to be spending a summer in Juniper again. The stars overhead seemed to wink at her as if they knew her secret but agreed that she was far, far too good to spend her best years sequestered in an ugly place like Culver City, forced to take a job in a boutique or— nightmare of nightmares—a *mall*.

She sat up when she heard Violet mutter the magic words "after party." Somewhere in that sentence, Seneca also thought she heard "The Shed."

Yeah, baby.

A nice vodka tonic in The Shed's intimate lounge area, relaxing against the cushions with her legs crossed and oh-so-casually waiting for guys who attended Brown and Yale to introduce themselves to her and tell her about their afternoon mountain bike rides, or how they were spending next weekend in Vegas before going back to L.A. for a few weeks to see their rich parents . . . perfect.

"I'm up for it," Seneca managed. "Whaddya say, Dahlia? It's only one thirty." And Seneca definitely wanted to keep going. She had to make up for all the parties she'd missed since she and Mom moved out of Axel's last Fourth of July. Besides, even if she were exhausted, the last thing she wanted was to go back to that damn log cabin and spend the night with her boring roomies. They were probably busy reading about the history of King's Crown or something. Trying to memorize trail maps or where all the tennis courts were situated so they could be extra-helpful to guests once their jobs officially started after orientation tomorrow.

Claire had potential. She hadn't shown up yet, but according to the paperwork she was a local, which meant her family could afford to live here year-round. On the other hand, Drew seemed like a carbon copy of every girl Seneca had ever met from the Midwest. The kind of girl who *belonged* in a flyover state. Intelligent, passably cute, and dedicated to either her classes, her clueless friends, her backwards-ass boyfriend, or her stupid high school athletic team (which was clearly Drew's focus, given the three pairs of running shoes and the tacky gray sports bra she'd left on the bedroom floor), but socially inept and with horrid taste in clothes.

At least Seneca had arrived at King's Crown first, so she could snag the best bed in the open bedroom on the cabin's second floor. Drew and Claire would have to fight to see who was stuck with the bed by the bathroom door and who was stuck with the one at the top of the stairs, where they'd be awakened by anyone going up or down.

Though, come to think of it, they probably didn't think about those practical things like Seneca did.

"I'm not sure," Dahlia said, giving Violet a look Seneca wasn't sure how to read. "I'm kind of wiped, and I have to be up early tomorrow. Mom's going to brunch at Adele Menyon's place and I've been invited along."

Seneca wanted to argue but kept her mouth shut. Dahlia had talked about becoming a TV journalist ever since she was twelve years old and met Diane Sawyer at an event Mr.(and their mom, the first Mrs.) Koss hosted at Mastro's Steakhouse. If Seneca blew Dahlia's chance to kiss up to Adele Menyon, the weekend NBC news anchor, for an internship, Dahlia would never forgive her.

Ten minutes later, with only a slight buzz left from the booze, Seneca made her way from the parking lot toward the front door of the main lodge. Unfortunately, Dahlia and Violet trailed right behind, claiming they needed to meet their mother in the lobby to discuss logistics for brunch.

According to Violet, their mother was staying at King's Crown for the week rather than at the Koss family's summer home fifteen miles outside of town— since the second Mrs. Koss was there with Mr. Koss— trying to knock off five to ten pounds before she went sailing with her new boyfriend (though the fact the perpetually rail-thin Mrs. K. thought she needed to lose five to ten was astounding to Seneca).

Seneca cursed under her breath. She hadn't counted on having the Koss sisters around the resort for anything more than the occasional meal. Pretending to be a guest just got a little more difficult, for the next week at least.

A uniformed doorman opened the resort's front doors, and Seneca faked left, as if she were headed for the concierge wing of guest rooms. But at that very moment, Dahlia stated—in a voice that could be heard by anyone within thirty feet—that Seneca was headed in the wrong direction. Their mother had spotted Seneca that morning walking on the path toward the employee cabins, so shouldn't Seneca be going to the lodge's back door? Dahlia even noted, with a wicked lilt in her voice, that Mrs. K. had seen Seneca beg to be given a ride into town in the van reserved for guests, and the driver had allowed it "even though she's a summer employee."

Seneca stifled a groan as Dahlia and Violet giggled, then walked ahead of her to air-kiss their mom, who had been sitting in a leather chair on the opposite side of the lobby, near the huge stone fireplace. But before Seneca could even walk over and say hello to Mrs. K. the sisters waved her off, a clear *We're done with you now, good-bye.*

Oh, God. How much did they know? Had they been toying with her all night?

And what about that Frankie guy?

Seneca gave them a dismissive wave in return, squared her shoulders, and strode toward the lobby's rear doors, the ones that led to her cabin. She'd figure out something to tell them tomorrow. Something that would make it look like *she* was the one who was totally cool for working there and that they were the losers for sitting on their skinny asses all summer. Maybe she could make it sound like a Paris Hilton/*The Simple Life* kind of gig, but not so passé.

How was it that vapid girls like Dahlia and Violet were born to brunch with celebrities and hardly even appreciate it, while she was living in an employee cabin, working her tail off to network with the right people so her mom, who actually *could* act, might get a job?

The whole situation boggled the mind. Someday, fate would fix things, Seneca was certain. Good people always won in the end, didn't they? Look at Hillary Clinton. All that crap from reporters about her hair and clothing tastes, all the embarrassment of having her husband cheat with an intern half her age . . . and who ended up with the Senate seat, a bestselling book, and invitations to all the best parties?

If things could come around for Hillary Clinton, they were sure to come around for Seneca Billeray. Seneca knew she had infinitely more style than Hillary, and more brains than Dahlia and Violet put together.

She wiggled her key in the cabin's door lock. It took three tries and a few words her Kansas roomie had probably never heard, but she finally got it open. Of course, not a single light was on and Seneca could hear snoring coming from upstairs.

Her dear, sweet roomie would probably be up bright and early, making all kinds of noise while she put on her smelly running shoes and her high-tech, sweat-wicking shirt and butt-ugly shorts.

"Ow!" Seneca swore aloud as her foot connected with something solid, then pulled off her Stuart Weitzmans and rubbed the injured spot. Must be Drew's dumbbells. She'd probably left them near the bottom of the stairs on purpose.

"Who's there? Seneca?" Drew's sleep-filled voice came from upstairs.

"No, a rapist," she hissed, still ticked off about smacking her foot. Didn't Drew think to leave on a nightlight or something, assuming that Miss Kansas wasn't malicious enough to have left the dumbbells there on purpose?

"Seneca?" Drew was louder this time. "That you?"

"Of course it's Seneca!"

"What were you doing out so late? We have orientation tomorrow morning. We have to be up in five hours."

"Omigosh, thanks for the reminder, Drew! I'd, like, completely forgotten that was tomorrow or I never would've stayed out so late!" Seneca kept her voice light enough that Drew wouldn't know for sure if she was being sarcastic, but made a face as she climbed the stairs. Drew would never grasp the importance of spending a night making nice to people like Dahlia and Violet Koss, so why bother with an explanation?

Besides, Seneca was happy. The Koss sisters might've treated her like dirt at the lodge, trying to put her in her place, but they wouldn't have hung out with her all night—or told that Frankie guy that he wasn't good enough for her—if they didn't still find her friendship one they needed to nurture. They wouldn't have bothered to jerk her around. She'd known them long enough to know they'd have ignored her entirely.

They'd wanted to be seen with her.

Seneca tiptoed into the tiny bathroom and closed the door—a little louder than necessary, but it wasn't as if Drew weren't awake already—then dropped her purse to the floor and reached to click on the light. Just before her hand hit the switch, she froze.

Her cell phone was still in the backseat of Violet's BMW. It hadn't fit in her purse, so she'd set it on the seat beside her.

She had to go get it. Violet hadn't put the top up, so she should be able to reach in and grab it, no problem. No way did she want the Koss sisters to find it first. What if they scrolled through the menu to see who she'd been calling since she'd arrived in Jupiter—or who'd called her—and found nothing?

She hobbled down the stairs, yanked on her shoes, then sprinted—well, as fast as she could in her heels and with her foot sore from kicking the dumbbells—along the path and into the lobby. Neither the sisters nor Mrs. K. were anywhere to be seen. As quickly as she could without looking obviously panicked, she walked through the front doors and toward the parking lot.

Too late. Violet was leaning against the back of her BMW, flirting outrageously with Todd Mirelli, a local Seneca had met last summer when he'd been dating Ashley Conrad, whose mom was a partner in a television production company that specialized in home and gardening shows. Todd's parents owned a 51 percent stake in the Juniper Mountain ski area. Naturally, he was one

of the wealthiest kids in town and one of the most connected. He knew town residents, skiers, and, since he'd
been dating Ashley, celebrities from all backgrounds . . .
everyone.

In that moment Seneca just *knew*. That's what the
look in the car had been all about—the one Dahlia shot
Violet before giving Seneca that whole Adele Menyon
spiel. And it was nothing more than that. A spiel. Adele
Menyon probably wasn't even in town.

They were going to The Shed all along and they'd
intentionally ditched her before hooking up with Todd,
whom Dahlia once confided was the guy Violet wanted, if
he ever dumped Ashley Conrad.

Seneca swallowed hard, then took a few steps backward, where the stone columns and high timbers of the
entryway would obscure the girls' view of her, should
they look over. A few minutes later Todd climbed into
the rear seat of the BMW, laughing aloud at something
Dahlia said from the front.

Violet revved the engine, then accelerated toward town.
A hyena-like howl erupted from the car's occupants, and
Seneca saw something fly from Dahlia's hand.

After the car's taillights were out of sight, Seneca
pulled her shoulders back—just in case anyone else was
lurking in the lot—then walked with as much confidence

as possible to where she'd heard the sound of metal striking asphalt, knowing what she'd find.

Yep. Dahlia had thrown the cell phone out of the car.

She palmed the phone and strode back to her cabin, where she flopped on the bed fully clothed. Who were they to do this to *her*? How dare they make her feel bad?

Her mother was Jacqueline Billeray, after all. She had an Academy Award, and she still (mostly) had her looks.

What *skanks*.

For all their money and social notoriety, the Koss girls weren't as hooked into Hollywood as some of the other teens who made appearances in Juniper every summer. The ones like Ashley whose parents were producers or studio execs. The ones whose parents ran the biggest talent agencies and might work hard for Jacqueline Billeray, if they could steal her away from her current agent.

The ones Seneca would hang out with from now on.

She pushed off the bed with its cheap sheets and tiptoed to the bathroom. After blowing her nose, she cinched her hair off her face with a white terrycloth band, tore the corner off a small pink foil pack, then dispensed a dime-size amount of anti-acne, anti-aging formula onto her ring finger. Thank goodness on her last trip to New York she'd managed to finagle a bagful of free samples from the women behind the various makeup counters at Henri Bendel. Promising to pass them along to her mom had gotten her enough to last the summer, as long as she didn't waste any.

She'd look better in ten years than the hard-partying, chain-smoking Koss girls. Patience and diligence would pay off. They'd regret treating her the way they had tonight. By then she'd be too busy with her own fabulous life to care.

She used her ring fingers to gently smooth the gel over her face, then smiled at her own glowing reflection.

Perfect.

She was *back*.

❋❋❋ FOUR *❋❋❋*

Marla must've dilly-dallied at the coffee shop. Not that Claire was dying to see Marla's moley face, but sitting in tightly packed metal folding chairs in the stuffy resort conference room with forty other teenagers—most of whom appeared to have stayed out late last night learning their way around the clubs of Juniper—sucked rocks.

Far worse, however, was the itchy discomfort of knowing you were being stared at by two girls sitting in the back row.

Juniper kids didn't usually work at King's Crown for the summer—most worked at their parents' businesses—so Claire hadn't expected to see any of her classmates here. Especially not two girls who belonged to Teen Jam. She'd loved what the minister had to say on her first two visits, but the kids . . . well, they hadn't been quite so welcoming. Not that they'd been out-and-out rude. They'd been perfectly polite, but in a way that made her think they were simply tolerating her presence and secretly hoped she'd go away.

Claire did a quick inventory of empty chairs, wondering if there was a way to change her seat without being obvious, but to no avail. Every single one was either occupied by a lounging teenager or had a plate and juice glass on it to hold someone's spot.

An older, buffed-up guy in a green King's Crown polo walked to the podium at the front of the room, flailed with the mic—he didn't seem to realize it needed to be switched on—then told everyone his name was Hud and announced that due to a glitch with the copy machine, orientation would begin in ten minutes. In other words, a full twenty-five minutes after the "promptly at nine" Marla had insisted upon.

A groan went through the room. Claire glanced toward the breakfast buffet set up on a long table by the back wall, snatched the empty glass she'd put on the floor, then picked her way through the crooked line of folding chairs, trying not to step on anyone.

The two girls in the back row started whispering, their hands covering their mouths but their eyes tracking Claire as she walked.

How obvious could they be? It was *sooo* Christian of them, too. She deserved a bagel along with a refill on her

OJ for enduring this without staring back at them or saying something nasty. Like telling them just how much their clothing taste sucked.

She'd left home at seven this morning just to make certain she arrived with plenty of time to check into her cabin, meet her roommates, and unpack—well, and to get out of the house early enough to avoid an are-you-sure-about-this scene with Mom and Dad. Unfortunately, neither roommate had been around when Claire let herself into the cabin with a timid hello, or even by the time she'd tucked the last of her clothes into the one empty bureau drawer they'd left her.

They were going to have to have a serious discussion about space sharing tonight. Maybe they'd assumed that, as a local, she'd keep most of her stuff at home. But leaving her only one drawer out of seven? So not right.

A runway-skinny, dark-eyed brunette wearing pricey pink yoga pants, matching pink sneakers, and a fake (but quality fake) tan sauntered through the double doors to the conference room and into the buffet line. Claire handed her a plate, then got in line behind her.

The brunette—who Claire figured for a hoity-toity type, like the women who came to Summit SuperSport and shopped with more concern for the fashion statement they made with their ski equipment than its functionality—picked up a pair of metal tongs and wrinkled her nose at the muffins and bagels. Lifting one at a time, she inspected them, then plopped them on the edge of the platter.

"Jesus Christ, but this blows," she muttered. "This is some nasty-ass stuff."

She didn't mean it, God. Claire shifted from one foot to the other, then sent more apologies heavenward as Hoity-Toity shoved another muffin aside with a grumble about high sugar and bad carbs.

A guy who looked about her age ambled into line behind Claire. After a few seconds of waiting with a plate tucked under his arm, he glared down the line, saw Hoity-Toity doing her bagel inspection, and told her to hurry it up—though he used language Claire hadn't heard since the last time she got plowed with Aaron and his friends at Tabby's Bar and the bouncer threatened to toss them out for being underage.

Wow, had that been only a few months ago?

Hoity-Toity shrugged and continued her picking, which resulted in the guy slamming his plate down. Four other teenagers who'd gotten into line behind him made faces.

Let her choose something or give up already. Please, God? She doubted it'd happen—the girl didn't even seem to care that she'd arrived fifteen minutes late—but another minute of this griping from both directions and Claire'd tell somebody to shut the hell up. She didn't want to start her summer of enlightenment by swearing at her coworkers.

"No fiber. No protein." The girl dropped the tongs as if the food had mold, then cursed in the general direction of the platter. "How do people live on this?"

Apparently Hoity-Toity *didn't* live on it or she wouldn't be so thin.

"Try down there." Claire pointed to a fruit tray at the end of the table. "The cantaloupe's pretty good."

"Huh?" The girl turned toward her, acting like she hadn't even noticed Claire following her through the line. "Oh. Thanks."

She started to turn away, then stopped and looked back at Claire, which held up the line yet again. "Is that Tory Burch?"

"Huh? Who?"

"Your top. Is it Tory Burch? It's stunning."

"Oh. Yeah." Claire fingered the fabric. She'd spotted it in the store window of a Juniper boutique when she was out walking with Aaron over spring break. Of course Hoity-Toity would recognize it. It cost a fortune—money Claire would have spent on a smokin' pair of skis instead of one flimsy scrap of fabric—but Aaron went back to the store and bought it as a surprise. And she had to admit, she felt fabulous in it.

"It's a great color on you, especially with your blond hair." She shot Claire a grin that said Hoity-Toity took her to be a kindred fashion spirit, then took a step toward the fruit tray and frowned. "I'm guessing the cantaloupe's not organic?"

"I'm not sure. I think it's Colorado-grown, though. It tastes really fresh." *And you oughta take it before the people in line get any more irate.*

The girl grabbed a cantaloupe cube and popped it in her mouth, said something that sounded like "yummers," then piled up her plate.

"I'm Seneca," she said, looking sideways at Claire.

"Oh." This summer really was going to be a test from God. How many Senecas could there be in the world? "In that case, I think you're my roommate. I'm Claire. Claire Watts."

"Yeah? You're Claire? That's great!" Seneca's entire look—the attitude, the straight dark hair, the shape of her face—reminded Claire of Shannen Doherty on those old reruns of *Charmed*. Seneca was exactly the type of person Claire had been hanging out with since she and Aaron hooked up. At least, until she realized how stupid the whole Juniper party circuit could be. It'd been tons of fun—*tons*—but it'd cost her more than she'd have thought possible.

Claire grabbed half a bagel—ignoring Seneca's frown at the choice—and a few more cubes of cantaloupe. As Claire tucked a napkin under her plate, Seneca said, "You're from here, right? Your profile said you live in Juniper all year."

"Yep."

"Cool. I bet you know all the best places to hang out." She gave Claire a head-to-toe perusal, then said, "I've heard there are a few parties tonight near downtown"— she rolled her eyes on the word—"or whatever you call the middle part of Juniper. It's not really big enough to be a real downtown like L.A. or New York, is it? Anyway, want to come with me and check 'em out? Everyone who's anyone is rolling back into town for the summer season, so it should be a blast."

"Um, I already have plans for tonight. My boyfriend's flying in." Thankfully, a true statement. Aaron's plane was probably touching down at DIA this minute. "Maybe another night?"

"Definitely."

Shoot. Seneca's *definitely* was way too peppy. It assumed too much. Claire quickly turned away from the buffet, grabbed a fresh juice, then headed back through the closest row of folding chairs to find an empty seat before Seneca said anything else. Why did she have to tell Seneca "maybe another night" when she knew she couldn't do that anymore? Even if she didn't drink, the temptation was at every bar and every party in town.

It would be so, sooo easy to fall into her old habits. To hang out with Seneca, get ripped out of her skull, and dance and dance with Aaron until neither of them could stand up any longer.

"Hi, Claire. Decided to come sit with us, huh?"

Claire stopped. How had she ended up walking toward the Teen Jam girls? Panicked by Seneca's offer to walk on the wild side, that's how. She stole a peek down the row. No more empty chairs down there. She might be able to step into the row in front of them, but an outdoorsy-looking girl with a blonde ponytail and serious muscles running down the front—and the *back*—of her arms looked like she was about to take the last empty seat there.

How much time in the gym did arms like that take?

Claire gave the Teen Jam girls a smile she hoped appeared sincere. "If that's okay."

The two girls shrugged, so Claire took the empty seat next to them. Immediately, Seneca dropped into the seat on the other side of Claire. Must've followed her from the buffet.

Shit.

I mean shoot, God. Shoot! I'm sorry!

Would she ever be able to keep from swearing in her thoughts? It was the same as saying it aloud, at least according to the youth minister at Teen Jam. God knew your innermost thoughts and He wanted you to keep your thoughts as pure as your actions. Maybe by the end of the summer she'd be better at it. Didn't it say in *Seventeen* last month that it took three to four weeks of constant effort before you could break a bad habit for good? Maybe it worked the same way with changing your thinking.

The Teen Jam girl in the seat immediately next to her—Claire remembered her name was Amanda—flipped a chunk of black hair over her shoulder and asked, "So how come you're working here?"

The other girl from Teen Jam, a near physical clone of Amanda, locked her gaze on Claire's face, completely intent. "Yeah, don't you usually work for your parents? You know, selling fancy tents and fishing poles to people who'll never use 'em?"

Claire took a sip of her juice, then twisted in her chair enough to face them without totally turning her back on Seneca. "I decided to do something different this year."

"Why?" This from the clone.

"Delia and I have been really curious," Amanda added.

So the clone's name was Delia. Hadn't there been a girl in her Trig class named Delia who just moved to Juniper last summer? Maybe the same girl. Claire hadn't paid much attention to anything in Trig last year.

"Well, I guess I—"

"Excuse me!" The blast of sound came at them like a wave from the front of the room. Marla, her mouth millimeters from the mic, added, "Come on, people, we're running behind! Eyes front! I need your undivided attention for the next ninety minutes, then we'll get you to your individual assignments."

Thank you, God. Who knew she'd be so grateful for an interruption from Marla?

While the buff guy who'd spoken earlier passed out three green King's Crown polo shirts to each summer employee, Marla proceeded to talk them through detailed maps of the property to the point that even the most directionally challenged person in the room got it. This was followed by a preschool-level lecture about the need to show up on time, the importance of good grooming, and an actual demonstration of the proper way to greet guests that included three separate requests not to chew gum or tobacco while on the job. (Though Claire wondered:

Did anyone other than professional baseball players or NASCAR drivers really chew tobacco? Ick!)

By the fifteen-minute mark nearly a dozen of the teenagers in the back rows of the room had pulled cell phones out of their pockets. Most were discreetly tapping out text messages, hiding their phones from Marla's view behind the chairs in front of them, but a few were openly playing games to kill time until they were able to leave for their work assignments.

Claire managed to make it forty minutes before slipping her own cell out to check for messages, which she figured made her the last person in the room to tune out Marla. Even Amanda and Delia had been sending notes back and forth on one of the orientation handouts.

The only person not messing around was Seneca. She'd fallen asleep as soon as the lights dimmed and Marla slapped the first overhead onto the machine.

Claire flipped open the cover on her pink leather cell phone case, then bit her lip to hold back a smile when she saw the screen.

```
got car srvc from DIA,
b thr 4 dinner w/ u
can't wait . . . luv u . . .
want u . . . A.
```

She quickly typed back:

c u 2nite . . .
luv u 4evr, C.

"So," Amanda said the instant Marla dismissed them and the lights came back on, rousing Seneca from her nap. "You never did answer my question."

Claire frowned. "Are you talking to me or Delia?"

"You, of course. You didn't need to suffer through that lecture for the sake of a summer job. Why work here when you could be at Summit SuperSport?"

Oh. *That* question. She tidied the pile of handouts in her lap, then stood as everyone began to file out of the rows and toward the doors.

"I thought it'd be good experience, I guess. I'm trying to"—How much should she say?—"I'm trying to move my life in a different direction. Meet new people, that kind of thing. I figured that it'd be good for me to do something other than work at Dad's store this summer. Get out of the house and live here instead."

Grow up now that God had forced her to realize that adulthood wasn't so far off. Putting on her friendliest smile, Claire asked, "Are you two in the employee cabins or are you living at home for the summer?"

"Home," they answered in unison.

"Oh. We'll probably still see a lot of one another, though."

Amanda glanced at Delia. The quick look said everything Claire needed to know—that the two Teen Jam girls had definitely been talking about her before orientation started, and that it hadn't been the kind of talk she'd like. She'd probably been the focus of the notes they'd been passing all through orientation, too.

"So, I have to ask." Delia set her empty plate down on the floor, then used the heel of her shoe to push it backward, under her chair, as she stood. "Why did you come to Teen Jam last month? We'd never seen you there before, and, um, it doesn't seem like it's your scene."

In other words, Claire mentally translated, *Why try to hang with our crowd when we know you spent both Christmas vacation and spring break smashed with your boyfriend? And why are you being nice to us now?*

That's probably why everyone there treated her like dirt. Not that it was very Christian of them, but Claire guessed she understood where they were coming from. "I went for the same reason everyone goes, I suppose."

"We go because we want to grow closer to God." Amanda's tone sounded just like Claire's English Lit teacher when he handed back graded essays and was disappointed with the results. "We don't go there to hook up with guys. So if you're just" —she used her fingers to make quote marks—"'looking to meet new people, that kind of thing,' Teen Jam isn't the place to do it. Stick with your rich Hollywood boyfriend and your party crowd for that."

Who in the world still made quote marks with their fingers? Not anyone Claire would want as a friend.

Except that she did.

"Look, I—"

"We're not trying to be mean, just honest," Delia added. "People like you don't just show up at Teen Jam, you know? If you're serious about developing a relationship with Jesus Christ, that's awesome. We'd love to have you come to our meetings. But don't ruin it for the rest of us if you're not serious. We don't want to be the target of whatever practical joke you and your friends are planning."

That's what they thought? What kind of awful bitch did they think she was? Or had she really been that awful?

Oh, shoot. Had she just thought the word *bitch*? She tried to look sincere as she focused on Delia. "Believe me, I'd never—"

An elbow jabbed into Claire's side. "What Hollywood

boyfriend? Is this the guy you said is flying in tonight?"

Amanda and Delia leaned forward, finally taking notice of Seneca, her clothes, and her too-good-to-be-true tan.

"I'm Seneca. Claire's roommate."

Delia's eyes widened a fraction. "Seneca Billeray, right? Your mom used to come here a lot. I saw her once last summer, when I was waitressing downtown. She was with that guy who lives in that monster house over on—"

"Oh, yeah. My mom knows everyone. Especially the crowd from L.A." She slid a glance at Claire. "So who's the boyfriend? I probably know him."

"Nobody," Claire said instantly. For one, she didn't care to have Seneca snooping into her personal life. And for two, who knew if Aaron would even *be* her boyfriend in a couple days?

"His name's Aaron Grey," Amanda volunteered, clearly not taking the hint. "His family bought a house here at the end of last summer. He's a real partier."

"But a nice enough guy," Delia added, though Claire knew it was only to soften Amanda's "partier" slam. Because coming from Amanda, it was definitely a negative character assessment.

"Girls?" Marla stood at the end of their row, giving them the same bossy look she'd given Claire in the parking lot the day before. "You need to get to your assignments. I thought I made that clear. We're already behind schedule. Miss Watts, I believe you should be going to the information desk? Miss Billeray, yoga studio. And you two" —she focused on Amanda and Delia while pointing a thick finger toward the lobby—"through there to the main dining room. You'll be shadowing the regular wait staff at lunch today."

Claire mumbled an apology and took the opportunity to bolt. Behind her, she heard Seneca mutter, "Aaron Grey? I swear I know that name. . . ."

Shit.

Shoot. Shoot, shoot, shoot.

* * * FIVE * * *

What a friggin' riot. Miss Hollywood dissed by the local girl, and the local girl dissed by the *other* local girls for being a partier. It was enough to make Drew laugh to herself while she stood at the back of the group of soon-to-be trail guides, listening to her new supervisor—the muscular guy who'd handed out the polo shirts at orientation—talk about what to expect on their first hike.

Drew figured going in that Marla's orientation would bore her almost as much as her bus trip had, but watching the spectacle while her two roomies held up the food line and then eavesdropping as they chatted behind her made the event worthwhile.

Seneca had been right about the horrible food choices— did anyone actually *eat* Danish for breakfast? Drew had always thought of Danish as slime-covered yellow paste on top of an oily croissant. Not in the least bit appetizing.

However, Seneca's wacky eating habits probably came from being a starlet wannabe, whereas for Drew, breakfast was all about choosing the best fuel for her body. The whole who-made-your-shirt conversation cemented Drew's impression of Seneca. Her roomie was flighty, stupid, and someone who cared about all the wrong things in life. Things Drew knew for a fact didn't matter a rip in the bigger scheme of things.

Of course, she felt bad for Claire, the girl with the Tory Burch top (whoever the hell Tory Burch might be). Claire seemed friendly enough—and Drew gave her credit for trying to ditch Seneca at the buffet table—even if Claire had obviously done something to piss off the other girls from her high school.

But Seneca? Listening to her try to make friends with Claire—and failing—gave Drew her morning dose of comedy. What cracked her up even more, though, was that Seneca didn't even freaking recognize her own *roommate* sitting in front of her and they'd had keys to the same cabin for nearly twenty-four hours. That's what Seneca got for sleeping all afternoon, then disappearing for half the night. Drew had left for an early morning strength-training session in the resort's gym before Seneca even woke up, and Miss Hollywood had been gone when Drew got back.

Predictably, Seneca had left a ton of hair and makeup products littering their tiny vanity. Drew had dumped them all on Seneca's bed. She made sure the lids were tight first, so nothing would be spilled, but she figured she'd made her point.

Girls who acted like they were entitled to every little thing pissed her off. It was nice to see a girl of that type have to go begging for one lousy friend. Drew couldn't imagine being that insecure.

Being alone was fine. Preferable most of the time.

Still, it'd be cool to find a friend and training partner here. Someone to push her harder so she'd get the most benefit possible from her summer training. Wouldn't be Claire, like she'd hoped. While Claire looked fairly athletic, Drew could tell she wasn't a runner. Plus, for whatever reason, Claire was apparently busy trying to find God.

But Rob . . . well, the more she thought about it, the more she believed Rob was a real possibility. Not so much because he had the body of a serious athlete and a gorgeous face, which Drew—studying him standing across the trail from her now—concluded he definitely possessed.

She'd simply learned over the last year that training with guys *worked*.

Girls could get all emotional on you if they didn't have a good run. Plus, girls were more likely to ease up on a training run if they wanted to jabber about their boyfriends, what their best friend said in Chemistry lab, or to spread the latest rumor. Couldn't run hard and get their gossip fix at the same time.

Even though most of the girls Drew trained with during the cross-country and track seasons back in Leavenworth were competitive, they weren't as dead set on not letting Drew beat them as the guys were. Guys always gave their runs that extra oomph just to be able to cross the finish line a few strides ahead of Drew. They didn't back off because they wanted to chat, because it wasn't "nice" to be aggressive, or, worst of all, because they felt sorry for you and your screwed-up home life.

She started winning events—and then broke that 2,000 meter record—because she started training with guys who didn't give a rat's ass about anything other than winning once their feet hit that starting line, whether they were at a state championship meet or Thursday afternoon practice.

Rob scooched along the back of the group of new guides until he was standing by Drew. Had he caught her studying him?

"Hey," he whispered, careful not to let Hud, who was

still speaking at the front of the group, hear him. "All this making sense?"

"Think so."

A few minutes later they took off for a group hike. Hud told them what they'd be expected to point out to guests along the way and gave them tips for recognizing when hikers were having trouble. They'd all have cell phones to call for assistance if anyone got injured, and tomorrow they'd all get CPR and basic first-aid training.

"You'll lead your first hike on Wednesday, with a veteran guide along to observe," Hud said. "They'll help out if you need it. By next week, you'll all be leading trail hikes on your own."

Rob stayed fairly close to Drew as the group followed one of the easy trails—the most popular one at the resort, Hud claimed, as he led them through the trees—but said nothing until they were nearly finished with the hike.

"What did you think?"

Drew couldn't help but smile at him. There was something about this guy that made her *want* to smile, even though she knew she looked butt-stupid when she smiled. Eleven years of appalling class photos didn't lie.

"Hud's cool. Seems like he's going to be a good person to have as a supervisor all summer."

Rob grinned. "I meant about the trail."

"Felt fine." Too easy to constitute a cardio workout, unfortunately. "I thought about running this one yesterday, but took the Divide trail instead. Wanted to get in a full three miles."

Hardest three miles she'd ever done. Adjusting to the altitude about killed her. By mile two she'd had to dial it down, despite the fact her adrenaline had been flowing fast when she'd left her horrid roommate behind on the sofa.

Training here might hurt her lungs for a few weeks, maybe make her feel a bit loopy, but it was all going to strengthen her.

"I figured you for a runner the way you were studying the trail map yesterday. Where are you from?"

"Kansas." She paused, then added, "Well, sort of. I'm an Army brat. My dad was stationed at Fort Leavenworth. My family's originally from West Virginia, but I've never lived there myself."

Rob nodded, taking it in. She could practically see the wheels in his mind spinning.

Geez, why didn't she shut up after the word "Kansas?"

"So you've moved around a lot?"

"Yeah."

"You said your dad *was* stationed at Fort Leavenworth. He's not now?"

"No." Proof she should've shut up. "How about you? Where are you from?"

"Denver 'burbs. Centennial."

"Oh." She'd heard of it but didn't know exactly where it was.

"Listen, I hope you don't mind," Rob said as they rounded the last corner in the trail and the resort's main building came into view, "but I asked Hud if I could be your partner for your first trail hike."

The guy moved fast. Maybe he wouldn't be such a good training partner. Flirting a little was one thing, especially since he was so gorgeous. But they'd be here for the whole summer. Why the rush?

He waved a hand in front of her face. "Hud. You know, the guy in front of us? Our boss? Directs the recreation programs? Doesn't have the foggiest idea how to work a microphone?"

"Oh, sorry." She must've looked blank there for a sec.

"Was there someone else you'd planned to go with you for your first official hike?"

"No. You'd be great. Thanks." If he turned out to be aggressive, she'd find a way to avoid him later. And it wasn't as if they'd be doing trail hikes together after the first few days. Even if they were working the same schedule—all summer employees would be given two days off a week, Marla had said this morning, just not the same two days—it wouldn't matter. He'd be taking his groups and she'd be taking hers, and they'd be on totally different trails. On her days off, she'd find a way to be busy if she needed to be.

Hud started talking again, giving them the rundown of what to expect during CPR and first-aid training. He also reminded those who'd worked the previous summer that they weren't exempt. Everyone needed to have the information fresh in their minds. "Guests do stupid things," he said. "They'll take a trail that's beyond their abilities or they'll have difficulty adjusting to the altitude. And then there are the random injuries even experts can sustain, like stepping on a rock the wrong way, sliding on a wet patch of soil—you catch my drift. You all need to be prepared."

He wrapped up by telling everyone they'd have a half hour for lunch in the employee cafeteria, then to meet him immediately afterward at the equipment shed to pick up the gear they'd need for the summer.

Rob didn't try to talk to her as they walked to the cafeteria. The other teenagers started introducing themselves to one another, chatting about where they'd come from, what jobs they'd held last summer. Like they needed to fill the mountain air with words.

Like they couldn't conceive of being around other people and just being quiet.

Drew stole a look at Rob as they entered the employee cafeteria through a thick pine door at the side of the building. He didn't seem nervous, as if he were trying to think of something to say. He just held the door open for her and followed her inside.

Unlike the fancy dining rooms for the guests, the employee cafeteria was strictly utilitarian. Serve yourself from the foods on the hot and cold buffet lines, grab a drink from the fountain area, find a seat at one of the long folding tables, then clean up your own mess.

A few of the full-time housekeepers occupied one table, but otherwise, the cafeteria was empty. Drew suspected, given the rumble in her stomach at the sight of food, that the hike had taken longer than it seemed and most of the other resort employees had already eaten.

She grabbed a plastic tray, then pushed it along behind everyone else as they surveyed the selections. She settled on a prepackaged salad topped with a generous dose of alfalfa sprouts and grilled chicken, a fat-free yogurt, a bag of pretzels, and a Diet Coke. There was plenty of crap available, what with triple-size chocolate chip cookies, congealed mac and cheese, and a plethora of hot dogs and hamburgers, but it looked—thankfully—

like she'd be able to find healthy choices. No more waxy-looking Danish.

She sat at the end of a long cafeteria table, happy that she'd snagged a spot with elbow room. Within seconds a girl asked to sit on her left and a guy Hud had pointed out as one of last year's guides sat across from her. Rob took the seat beside him, straight across from Drew.

As the table filled the buzz of conversation grew louder and louder. Drew focused on her salad, nodding when people talked but letting them drone on around her without moving to participate. Already they were yakking about which guides had hooked up with other resort employees at an impromptu get-together they'd had last night in one of the cabins.

She was mid-sip of her Diet Coke, straw in her mouth, when she felt Rob looking at her. Without thinking, she raised her head. He wasn't participating in the conversation, either. Just eating, letting the activity around him continue.

And grinning at her.

Not an overt grin, the kind where a guy is making dead sure you know he's into you. More subtle. As if they were the only two people in the room who didn't feel the urge to fill it with sound.

As if they were the only two people in the room, period.

Drew smiled back, even though the straw was still in her mouth, because no way was she the type to look away and let him believe he made her uneasy.

She set down the soda and continued eating in silence, other than when the girl next to her said something about Hud's coolness quotient and she was compelled to give an "um-hmmm" to indicate she was listening.

Rob kept right on eating his turkey on rye, casual as anything. When he finished, he leaned back to two-point the plastic wrap into an oversize gray garbage can near the wall. As the balled-up wrap left Rob's fingertips, he leaned farther back and his foot connected with hers beneath the table.

Shot made, he straightened and picked up his drink. His foot, however, didn't move. His instep rested against the outside of her foot.

Then she felt his other foot box hers in.

Drew's quads jerked; the muscles in her hamstrings contracted.

She needed to run. *Bad*.

❊❊❊ SIX ❊❊❊

Aaron Grey. Aaron Grey. Seneca let the name roll through her mind as she sat behind the front desk of the spa, pretending to pay attention to the spa director, who was sitting next to her demonstrating the computer system.

Why was it so damned familiar? She'd ask around (discreetly, of course) and figure it out. Aaron Grey had to be somebody or she wouldn't have the name stored in the recesses of her brain. Claire might act all casual, but no one wore Tory Burch and had a boyfriend flying in from L.A. if they weren't a person with all the right friends. And that, Seneca decided, was a very good thing for her.

But what was with Claire kissing up to those two gung-ho Christian types during orientation? That seemed way out of character, given everything else Seneca had observed about her new roomie. Those girls must have some dirt on Claire or something. It'd be interesting to know what.

"Seneca? Are you paying attention? You look a little sleepy."

What, the soft spa lighting, the Zen-like background music, and the bubbling of the wall-mounted copper fountain *weren't* supposed to put her to sleep?

"I'm listening." Seneca gave Kelsey, the spa manager, a smile that flashed the white, flawlessly aligned teeth for which Mom and Axel paid oodles of money. "I'm to have each hotel guest sign in with their name and room number, give them a towel and a robe, then walk them to the locker room and show them how the locker works."

"And offer them spring water."

"Of course!" Unless it was Dahlia and Violet coming in to take a yoga class with their mom. She'd be tempted to drop a saline laxative into theirs first.

The Koss girls were bound to make an appearance sooner or later—if not for a class, then they'd be right across the hall at the beauty desk inquiring about oxygenating facials and French manicures. With Mrs. Koss all crazy to drop pounds off her already sticklike frame, she was probably going to spend a lot of time in the spa. Where she went, Dahlia and Violet eventually followed. Good thing Mrs. K. was only staying here a week.

She had to find a way to turn this job to her advantage.

First step would be to avoid wearing one of those ugly King's Crown polo shirts all summer. She'd managed to steer clear today; none of the summer hires had to wear them until tomorrow. Tonight, she'd check the label to see if the shirt contained any fibers to which she could claim an allergy. In the meantime, maybe she could propose that spa employees wear something more spa-like to differentiate themselves. Like a cami and yoga pants.

But how to make it seem to the Koss girls—and to any other celeb clients, the ones she really needed to schmooze—like she was there for a good reason? Would they buy it if she simply said her mom thought it'd be good for her to work for the summer?

Ooh! Maybe she could claim her mother needed help prepping for a role, but that she was sworn to secrecy about the film. An indie project that delved into the lives of ordinary people working at a luxury resort. Though she'd need to make it sound like her mom wasn't too busy to take on another project. Preferably a big-budget project helmed by someone who couldn't stand Axel Randolph.

"And if someone comes in who isn't a resort guest?" Kelsey prodded.

Seneca leaned forward in her chair and pulled up a

menu on the computer. "I go in here and check for their name?"

"Almost. If it's for a massage or other appointment in the spa—reflexology, a body wrap, facial, that kind of thing—just walk them through the locker room to the treatment waiting area as you would for a hotel guest. Anyone can make an appointment in the spa for treatments. But if they're here for a meeting with a trainer, or to take a fitness class or use the gym, they need to be a King's Crown Club member. So you need to have them swipe their membership cards here," she said, tapping a small black scanner discreetly placed at the edge of the polished granite countertop. "The regulars will do it and keep walking. You won't need to show them the locker room or any of that. But if this beeps, it means either their membership has expired or the card's not reading. *Then* you need to ask them to hold on a sec while you look them up. Got it? No one can be admitted to the exercise facilities unless they're a current member or a hotel guest."

"Got it." Same as at every upscale gym. And Seneca was willing to bet a lot of people let their memberships expire, then begged to be let in for the day with promises to renew next time they came in. If so, she'd do them the favor and subtly hint that they could pull a few strings for her in return. Wasn't as effective as meeting someone during an evening out, where they could see that she was part of their social circle. But she'd take what she could get.

As long as she didn't look desperate. She'd have to watch that. Eau de Desperation turned off the movers and shakers faster than anything.

Kind of like living in a modest house in Culver City.

A noise at the spa's glass doors caught her attention. A wiry guy with light brown, all-over-the-place short hair and wire-rimmed glasses pulled when he should've pushed.

"Oh, you must be Jake!" Kelsey waved the guy over once he came through the double doors the proper way. "Marla called down to say you were going to be late. I was wondering what happened."

"She lost some of my paperwork. Had to redo it."

"Figured as much. Always happens to one or two people on the first day."

Seneca studied the new guy. She'd thought she would be the only summer hire in the spa area—most of the other teens were in food service or working outdoors as landscapers and trail guides—but apparently not. This guy looked like he'd never seen the inside of a spa in his life. Not with his vintage AC/DC concert T-shirt, baggy camouflage shorts, and flip-flops.

Eww. Did he have hair on his toes?

"Jake, this is Seneca." Kelsey glanced from Jake to Seneca and back. "Seneca's just finished learning the computer, so she can show you what's what while I go pick up the new shipment of massage oils from the receiving room."

Come again? The computer system didn't seem that tough so far—Seneca figured she'd pick it up as she went along—but that was a world away from being able to teach someone else how to use it.

Kelsey continued, "Seneca, Jake will be working the desk with you. He'll be escorting any male guests to their locker room while you're handling the women. I'll give him the run-through on that when I get back, but if the two o'clock massage appointment shows up before I get back, just tell Jake what to do, all right?"

"Um, sure. It's a guy coming in for the appointment?"

"A couple."

Kelsey slid past Jake, who was now standing at the edge of the counter, then strode to the glass doors. She reached for one of the sleek U-shaped handles, then paused and spun around. "Oh, and tomorrow, you two need to wear your King's Crown shirts. You got them at orientation, right? Those let guests know that you're a go-to person here in the spa. Wanted to remind you because I'm sure I'll forget later. And nice pants for both of you, no shorts." She grinned at Seneca. "I bet the green shirt looks good on you. It's your color."

With that, Kelsey disappeared down the long hallway connecting the spa to the main resort building, leaving Seneca alone with Jake.

"She's full of energy." Jake swiped a hand through his hair, leaving it even worse off than before.

"Yeah. And bad fashion sense."

He gave Seneca a head-to-toe perusal. "I don't see you as the green polo shirt type. I know I'm not." He dropped into the black office chair Kelsey had been using, then rolled over to where Seneca was sitting. "So how complicated is this thing?"

Seneca clicked back to the main menu, then glanced sideways at Jake. *Wow.* Really cute guy, if you could overlook the toe hair. Now that he was up close she saw that he had the softest, most expressive green eyes behind his glasses, and, with an introduction to a comb, his hair could be genuinely sexy.

And he smelled like he had just showered, unlike that Frankie guy at the bar.

She tried to focus on the computer screen. "Honestly? I was only sorta paying attention while she showed me 'cause it seemed pretty easy. But don't tell Kelsey I said that."

Jake crossed his arms over his chest and leaned back in the chair. "Not a problem. So give me what you know."

Seneca ran through the basics, surprising herself with her ability to figure everything out. Usually she wasn't the organized type, but the system seemed intuitive to her.

"Makes sense to me," Jake said when she finished. He stretched to pick up a piece of orange paper from the desk. "This the schedule for exercise classes or something?"

Seneca nodded. "Kelsey says there's a new one each week. Guests get it when they check in, but we keep a copy here so we can refer to it if someone has a question. If you flip it over, it explains the classes."

"Good, because something called Pumping Bodies sounds X-rated."

Seneca reached over to steal the sheet out of Jake's hand. "No way! That's a scream. Gotta be a class with weights." She located the explanation, then ran a finger beneath it to show Jake. "Yep. It says 'an hour-long, high-energy class combining weights and cardio work. Bring a towel and large bottle of water for this one. You're gonna sweat.'"

"Lemme see." Jake rolled his chair another few inches, bumping it into Seneca's, then grabbed the sheet back.

Was he flirting?

"What else do these rich people do when they come to a spa? Budokon, whatever that is. Energy Supersprint. Bikram Yoga. Oh, here we go! Goddess Yoga. Give me a freakin' break. Apparently, if you're loaded, your yoga is just that much better than everyone else's. Can't have any ordinary person yoga, uh-uh. Gotta be the *goddess* kind."

"Hey, some of those classes sound good." Goddess Yoga, especially. She'd taken an early morning stretching class before going to orientation, since free classes—space permitting—were an employee benefit. It'd been relaxing, especially after a night listening to Drew snore, but Goddess Yoga sounded intriguing. And yoga was fantastic for keeping you strong without making you all bulky. *Bulky* was not a word Seneca ever wanted to have associated with her figure.

"Maybe," Jake admitted. "But you won't catch me in there. It'll be entertaining to see who shows up to take these classes, though. Maybe Kevin Costner will come by. I heard he stayed here for a couple weeks last summer to get in shape for a movie role."

"Yeah, I heard that, too." From her mom, who'd tagged along with Axel to meet Kevin for lunch in town when the two men were batting around the idea of joining forces on a film.

A film Jacqueline wouldn't be starring in. Not that Axel would have wanted her to, anyway. Not if it meant her being away on location.

Seneca tapped a few keys on the computer, trying not to dwell on how her mom had let a jerk like Axel derail her career. This was one of those times she wished she had a real father, instead of a tattered copy of *People* from the week she was born talking about how Jacqueline Billeray had a new baby daughter courtesy of an anonymous donor at a sperm bank.

Then again, a real father might've turned out to be just as big an asshole as Axel.

"So let's see who's scheduled for spa appointments today. Anyone getting their hair or nails done goes across the hall to the beauty salon, but I bet they'll be listed here in the computer right alongside the appointments for spa treatments."

"Huh," Jake said, leaning over her shoulder to get a better look at the screen. "No one I recognize. But I'm not tuned in to this stuff the way most people are."

Seneca scrolled down the list. As she moved the mouse, the back of her arm bumped against the front of Jake's. "Sorry," she mumbled.

But *whoa*. Just how much muscle did he have under that AC/DC shirt?

"So how'd you end up working in the spa?" she asked.

She felt him shrug behind her. "This is my fourth summer here. Did landscaping the last three years, but I told them I wanted something indoors this time around. Guess they have a hard time getting guys to volunteer for spa duty. They'd rather be outside so they can get a workout. Or else work in the main restaurant so they can snag fancy food."

His *fourth* summer here? "You must be in college, then."

"I'm going to Boulder in August. Graduated from high school last week."

"Here in Juniper?" If he'd worked here that many summers, maybe he was a local. He might not be dialed in to who was who, but that didn't mean his parents weren't. "I think it'd rock to live here all year."

He leaned back in the chair, crossing his arms over his chest. "I go to Juniper High, but my family lives down the mountain, in a smaller town called Caseyville. My parents both work in Juniper, though, so I started working at King's Crown before I got my license because I could get rides to and from work with them. You know the Exxon right as you come into town? My dad owns and manages that station. Mom helps out sometimes, but her regular job's at Peak Souvenirs. One of those places that sells everything from postcards to snow globes to locally made belts and purses."

"Cool." But not really. Too bad, because Jake himself seemed pretty cool.

Jake directed Seneca's gaze toward the large black and white clock over the doorway. "It's almost two. No Kelsey. Think she'll show up first, or the couple coming in for the massage?"

"Dunno. Let's see if they're resort guests. I think I can figure that out."

She scrolled back up to the beginning of the appointment file, then looked at the massage schedule. "Two o'clock. Elliott and Judy Grey. They're not guests—Kelsey says that guest names show up in green instead of in black. But the box is checked saying they're members of the King's Crown Club, so they'll probably know their way around the locker rooms. You won't have to do anything."

"Good." He looked past her, studying the screen. "I think you're on tomorrow, though. It says Tuesday at the top."

"Oh. Duh." She moved the mouse to click back to Monday, but paused with her finger over the button.

Elliott and Judy *Grey*?

Elliott Grey was one of the best-known directors in

Hollywood—not just because he'd won a Best Director Golden Globe a few years back, but because he was also the cofounder and CEO of Grey Tower Productions, a company with its fingers in tons of solid projects. She'd seen blurbs in *Variety* about deals being made by Grey Tower Productions more times than she could count. This could be a different Elliott Grey, but how likely was that?

Did he live in Juniper? Surely she'd have heard about him being here if he did. He was one of the few people in Hollywood who had as much pull as Axel Randolph. One who wouldn't care about whether Axel blacklisted an actress like, say, Jacqueline Billeray.

Seneca clicked through a few more screens to find their initial membership date. Sure enough, the Grey family joined the club at the end of last summer and a notation in the comment box said they'd just bought a home in Juniper.

Seneca bit her bottom lip without thinking. Nothing her fave Kinerase lip treatment wouldn't fix. Talk about hitting the jackpot. How lucky could she get? If the Greys just moved to Juniper at the end of the summer, they might have missed a lot of the gossip about Mom and Axel's breakup.

"Gotta check out Elliott and his wife tomorrow,

though," Jake said as Seneca clicked onto the Monday schedule and searched for the two o'clock appointment. "You have to be from a family with money, power, or both if you're named Elliott, or you'd get your ass kicked whenever the rowdy kids got bored at school. I'm guessing if the guy can afford to be a member of the club and hang out in the spa, he has the money part."

Seneca grinned. Okay, working with Jake might be fun.

If she was going to be stuck working forty hours a week, she might as well enjoy the company, right?

She slid a glance at Jake. "If it's the Elliott Grey I'm thinking of, he has the power part, too."

And apparently he had a son named Aaron. A son who'd probably be spending a lot of time with his girl-friend, Claire, right in Seneca's very own cabin.

*** seven ***

"Hey, anyone here?"

The silence following Seneca's question didn't surprise her. Who wanted to be in a musty cabin at five p.m. after their first day at work?

She tossed her pink Pumas onto the rag rug fronting the cabin's scuzzy brown couch. Jock Girl was probably lifting weights or running—again—and Claire was out doing whatever she needed to do to get ready for Aaron Grey.

Hopefully, part of Claire's plans included bringing Aaron back here later tonight. Once Seneca met him, things would be fabulous. Drop her mother's name while she hung out with him and Claire and, before she knew it, Mom would be cast in a small but important role for a Grey Tower flick that *Variety* would refer to as a comeback. Maybe they'd even call Mom a possible Best Supporting Actress contender. Then, voila! No more resale shop threats.

Seneca clicked the television on and flipped through a few channels before she settled on HGTV. Nothing like a high-end house tour to get her spirits up. Because contrary to what she'd told Claire at orientation that morning, she had no parties to attend, nowhere to go. Just a date with HGTV and *Homes Across America*, at least until she met Aaron Grey and whoever else Aaron and his parents might be socializing with for the summer.

She flopped onto the couch, causing a surge of dust motes to take to the air.

Ewww. She brushed off her fave pink yoga pants. Where was Melanie when you needed her? She'd have aired out the cushions, vacuumed them, and worked whatever magic she knew to get every last bit of odor out of the fabric if this had happened back home. Seneca had never had to deal with dust at home in L.A.

Well, not until Mom had to let Melanie go.

How in the world was she going to stand living in this shack all summer? Okay, when she connected with Elliott Grey, it'd be worth it, but in the meantime it sucked. When Jake said something this afternoon about what to expect for her first paycheck in a couple weeks—and she realized he was serious—she almost choked on her cantaloupe over how little money she'd be making.

Mom might've insisted she get a job so she could

cover her own expenses for the summer, but who could live on this kind of income? How could she not have thought to ask about the money before agreeing to come out here?

Because she'd assumed a hot resort like King's Crown would pay well, that's why. But no, it'd take a week's salary just to buy new shades and a decent pair of shoes.

Homes Across America started, the smiling host giving a teaser of the homes being toured. Seneca rolled her eyes. Rerun. She'd seen it twice, even. She clicked off HGTV, determined to use her downtime wisely.

Maybe she could try out that detoxifying masque sample she'd grabbed from the spa this afternoon. See if a brighter complexion perked up her mood. As a bonus, she'd look nice when—if—Claire brought her boyfriend back here later. Had to have the right look to indicate to Aaron that she should be at the top of the list if he had any get-togethers at his house on the weekends.

She'd searched the computer files until she located a Juniper address for the Greys in the member records. According to MapQuest, the Grey family's summer place was fairly close to Todd Mirelli's, which meant it had to be something else.

Who needed Dahlia and Violet's connections or a *Homes Across America* mood-booster when she could kill two birds with one stone by finagling an invite to Elliott Grey's house? And the Koss girls could kiss her ass if she happened to see them there.

Seneca reached over to her Stella McCartney bag, trying to remember where she'd tucked the samples of the cleanser, masque, and toner. As she flipped past the handouts that Marla had given out at orientation, a blinking red light near the television caught her eye.

They had an answering machine?

Maybe Mom had called. Discovered she had a stash of cash somewhere her accountant had overlooked. Or she'd had an audition that went really well. Seneca rolled off the couch, stepped over her bag, then hit the button on the machine.

Hi, Claire, it's Mom. Hope this is the right number—I asked the front desk people and they connected me here when I couldn't reach you on your cell. The machine just said cabin number nine when it picked up.

So the reason for my call . . . I was wondering if you had dinner plans for this Saturday night. The Mirellis are coming over for barbeque and I'd like you to be

here. Mrs. Mirelli said she hasn't seen you
over there with Todd and all your other
friends lately. She sounded bothered by
it. Did something happen? Are you not
hanging out with him as much anymore?
They've been good neighbors for the last
twenty years, so I'd hate to think you two
aren't getting along. But maybe Mrs.
Mirelli is imagining things.

Call me when you get this. And think
about Saturday, all right, sweetheart?
Love you!

"Well, well, well," Seneca whispered. Talk about
hitting it big at roommate roulette. Claire's family was
tight with the Mirellis?

Parties at Claire's might be just as good as attending
parties at the Greys'. She'd have to be extra-nice to
Claire. Good thing she liked her already.

The machine beeped and a second message began.
The voice was unmistakable. She'd heard it just last
night in the resort parking lot.

Hey, Claire, darlin'! Where are you hiding? Your mom
said you're working at King's Crown for the summer

instead of at the store. What's with that?

Anyway, sounds like your parents are having mine over for a cookout this Saturday. If you're back to being your normal self, want to go out somewhere with me afterward? Maybe tell me why you've been acting so strange the last couple months? Did I do something to piss you off? Was Ashley Conrad acting like a bitch to you when she was here for spring break? I broke up with her last month, you know. She was being clingy in the extreme. Didn't want me to hang with my friends, especially the female ones like you, even though she lives in freakin' L.A. and I told her I had no interest in anyone besides—

Hey, move it, already! The light's green!

Sorry, I'm calling from the car. Lost tourist in front of me.

By the way, I heard you went to a meeting with the God-is-my-homeboy crowd. Call and say it ain't so! Nothing Ashley said should have driven you to that. She can be hideous, but that's no reason to go looking for new friends. Your parents make you go or something?

Anyway, you've got my cell, right? Aaron's invited on Saturday too, if he's around. Tell him I said hey. Talk to you soon!

As Alice in Wonderland said, curiouser and curiouser.

The machine beeped again, acting like it wanted to play a third message, but there was only silence.

Thing was probably a decade old.

Seneca fumbled through her bag, finally putting her hands on the spa samples. As she started to zip it shut, an unfamiliar voice came from the machine.

> *Drew? Is this working?*
> *It's your mother.*

More silence.

Seneca walked over to the machine. It was still playing—she could hear some scratching noises now. Did the woman not know how to leave a message? Surely there were answering machines in Kansas.

> *I just wanted to check and make sure you're all*
> *right out there in Colorado. I know I said it'd be*
> *good for you to go, to get away from here for a*
> *while, but . . . it's just that I—*

"Hey! Mind your own business!" Drew reached past Seneca and punched a button on the machine, deleting the message and scaring Seneca out of her wits. How the hell could Drew be so loud when Seneca wanted to sleep, yet come in like a professional burglar now?

"Hey right back! I wasn't being nosy, just listening to the messages." Seneca took a breath to slow her heartbeat, then crossed her arms over her chest—a better chest than Drew's, she noticed, even though Drew's arms looked like those on the women who did stunt-double work on action flicks. How'd the girl get that ripped? A lot of actresses she knew would be jealous of those arms. "That was your Mom, Drew. You erased it and it wasn't even finished yet."

"What, so you could hear the rest? You'd have skipped it if you were just listening for your own messages," Drew pointed out.

"I didn't exactly study the buttons. I just hit play and let it roll." Seneca scowled at her. Even if it'd make her face wrinkly, Drew deserved a good scowl aimed in her direction. "What is your problem?"

"No problem. I just like my privacy, all right?"

"Fine. But if you don't mind me saying so, she sounded sad. She and your dad are probably lonely at home without you. You'd have heard that in her voice if you weren't so paranoid that I might be spying on you." Seneca uncrossed her arms and strode over to her bag, flipping it over her shoulder so she could go upstairs and get gorgeous before Claire showed up with Aaron.

"Believe me, I have no reason to want to spy on you."

A vein stood out on Drew's forehead. Ugly one, too. "I'm going to say this in as nice a voice as possible, Seneca. You need to butt out. We have to live together all summer long, and I'd rather not get started on the wrong foot. But my relationship with my mom—my family—is private. I don't want to discuss it."

"Gotcha. Hey, I'm sorry if I offended you."

Drew acted all tough—*looked* all tough, with her hiking shorts, her runner's legs, and her pulled-back blond ponytail—but something in the way she said *family* made Seneca think there was a lot about Drew that wasn't so tough.

She sounded the same way Seneca knew she sometimes did when she was trying to explain her father—and lack thereof—to anyone who needed it spelled out for them.

Defensive. Rehearsed.

"No harm, no foul," Drew muttered, then passed Seneca and took the stairs by twos up to the sleeping area.

Seneca rolled her eyes. Drew better not hog the bathroom.

She followed Drew—quickly, but not so that it'd look like she was trying to race her to the bathroom—then stopped short when she got to the top of the staircase.

Drew was already sitting on her bed, yanking off her hiking shorts (and exposing some seriously bland white undies), but that wasn't what caught Seneca's attention. Or made her temper flare.

"What in the hell did you do to my bed?" Seneca kept her voice one notch short of a scream. "You were in my stuff!"

"Oh, that?" Drew glanced at Seneca's bed and shrugged. She kicked her hiking shorts toward the laundry basket, then pulled on a pair of nylon running shorts. "I wasn't *in* your stuff. I *moved* your stuff. You left it all over the bathroom and it was in my way. Don't worry, nothing spilled."

Drew turned her back to Seneca, picked up her hiking shorts, then dumped them in the canvas laundry bag at the foot of her bed as if Seneca hadn't even spoken.

Screw Drew and her family issues, whatever they might be. The gloves were off.

First, this chick hits the window shade on purpose while I'm asleep on the couch, then leaves for a run without pulling it back down. Next, she dumps her dumbbells where she knows I'll trip on them. Then she bitches me out simply for listening to the answering machine. And now this?

Seneca tossed her bag onto her bed and grabbed Drew's running shoes from the floor.

"Hey—"

That got her attention.

"Maybe I'll just drop these out the window, since they're in my way. No harm, no foul, huh, Drew?"

"Oh, come on!"

"You wanna start off on the right foot? Then tell me: What kind of morons do they raise out there in Kansas?"

✳✳✳ EIGHT ✳✳✳

"Oh. My. God. You're calling *me* a moron?"

Claire took a step inside the door to her cabin, which someone had left ajar. Sure enough, the loud voices she'd heard while walking down the path—including the voice taking the Lord's name in vain—belonged to her roommates.

Not an auspicious start to the evening.

"There are *three* of us living here, Seneca." So the blasphemer must be Drew, the roommate she hadn't yet met. "Can you do math? That means you get one third of the space. Do you want me to show you how fractions work? Or do they not teach fractions in the schools in L.A.?"

Shoot. This was not what she needed right now. Aaron just called on his cell. His parents were unpacking and they'd given him the car for the evening. She only had thirty minutes to get ready to meet him for dinner and she had to look her absolute best. How was she going to manage that if she had to walk through World War III?

"You were already gone when I left for the gym this morning, okay, Drew? I figured you were all done in the bathroom. Next time, I'll clear it away."

"You? At the gym? What, to meet guys?"

"I had a stretching class."

Claire thought she heard a snort. A genuine *snort*.

"Just don't touch my stuff, all right?" It was clearly Seneca speaking. "That face cream you tossed on my bed cost more than your precious running shoes here. If we're going to get along, then we need to have a serious conversation about boundaries."

"And about how you're going to respect everyone else's?" Drew retorted. "If you can handle that, then we won't have any more problems. And I don't just mean with our stuff. I mean respecting each other's personal boundaries—like you not listening to my phone messages."

"I already told you, I didn't mean to—"

Claire paused, her hand still on the doorknob. So Seneca had already nosed into Drew's private life, just like she'd tried to butt into Claire's own private life by asking Amanda and Delia all about Aaron.

Great.

"Give me back my shoes, Seneca, and I'll happily get out of your way."

There was a loud thunk, as if Seneca had dropped Drew's shoes, then silence. Claire wondered when she should go upstairs. The clock was ticking; how could she possibly shower and get her hair dry in time?

She moved inside the doorway, but then Drew spoke again. "If you don't like me, fine. But when Claire shows up, try to be more considerate of her. At least give her another dresser drawer. I have two but you took four. Leaving her one drawer is *not* cool. All right?"

"Fine."

More silence. Claire counted silently to five, then took a few loud steps into the cabin and shut the front door with just enough force to be heard upstairs.

"Hey, anyone here?" The cheer in her voice sounded forced, but no way did she want them to know she'd overheard their fight. She needed to introduce herself to Drew, then grab the bathroom and get gorgeous. Hopefully without too many questions from Seneca.

"Up here," Seneca yelled.

Claire got to the top of the stairs just as Seneca entered the bathroom and shut the door.

A girl with a long blond ponytail—the one who'd sat in front of her at orientation, judging from the serious muscle tone in her arms—was sitting on the bed nearest the stairs, putting on a pair of running shoes. "You must be Claire," she said.

"Yep. You're Drew?"

She nodded as she finished tying her shoe and stood. "Hate to say hi and run, but, well . . . I'm going to the main lodge to pee and then for a run." In a quieter voice she added, "I think she's going to be in there a while. She has a beauty *routine*, and I'm not interrupting her."

Claire must have let her frustration show on her face, because Drew said, "If you've gotta pee, you can run up to the lodge with me. Marla left for the day, so we won't get lectured about using guest facilities."

"It's not that. I'm meeting my boyfriend in half an hour, and I haven't seen him since he was here for spring break. I got sweaty walking all over the grounds after orientation. They wanted me to see everything since I'm working at the information desk. Even though I live at this altitude, when it hits ninety in the mountains, it gets me all gross."

"No kidding." Drew's smile seemed genuine. Like it couldn't possibly be coming from the girl who was telling Seneca off only a couple minutes before. "I'm one of the trail guides. Sweat buckets this afternoon."

"And you're going out for a run now?"

"Crazy, I know." Drew shifted, raised her right foot behind her, then grabbed her ankle to stretch her right quad. "But I'm really close to breaking some state records, and I'm hoping that if I train hard this summer it'll pay off when school starts in the fall."

"When you've been hiking all afternoon, though? That's dedication."

Drew's shoulders hiked, then dropped. "You want something bad enough, you just do it, you know? Mind over matter and all those clichés. And I know if I concentrate and put in the hard work, I can do it."

"That's awesome," Claire said. If she spent the summer focusing her own efforts at being a good Christian the way Drew focused on her running, would she get the same results?

"You a runner by any chance?" Drew interlaced her fingers behind her back, then raised her arms. Her back made a popping sound, but Drew didn't seem to notice.

Claire shook her head. "I like to mountain bike, though. If you want to go sometime when we both have the day off, I can get you a bike and a helmet, easy."

"Really? I'd love that." Drew stretched her left quad, then whispered, "Tell Seneca to get her tail out of the bathroom if you need to get ready to meet your boyfriend. She's a total space hog if you don't grab your share. All right?"

Claire just nodded. Drew wished her good luck, rolled her eyes in the direction of the bathroom, then bounced down the stairs and out the door.

"Is she gone?" Seneca asked a minute later, sticking her face—a green face—out of the bathroom.

"Yeah. Hey, can I have the bathroom? I need to get ready."

Seneca stepped out and waved Claire inside. "No problem. Is your boyfriend on his way over?"

"I'm meeting him downtown."

Seneca's smile wavered. "Bummer. I'd hoped to meet him. Let him know it's cool with me if he wants to hang out with you here at the cabin. I'll get out of your way."

"Thanks. I'll let him know." But not anytime soon. Not just because Seneca's face was the color of a lime, or even because Claire had a niggling feeling about Seneca's level of interest. She'd chased Seneca types away from Aaron before and she knew she could do it again if necessary.

Claire needed to get things straight with Aaron first. *Alone.*

Her stomach pitched at the thought. Should she tell him what happened right away? Wait until after dinner?

After dinner would be safer. She needed to feel him hold her, to know that he still loved her. If she spit everything out first, they might never get to the hugging and kissing part she craved. And waiting until after dinner would give her time to gauge how he felt about her, what words she should use to tell him how awful the spring had been for her. And what she'd decided to do about it.

Plus, it'd be rude to drop something so heavy without getting him in a good mood first.

"Maybe we can all go downtown, find someplace to hang out," Seneca said. "Take Drew with us."

She wanted to take *Drew*? After what Claire had just overheard?

Seneca waved in the direction of the lodge. Through the window, Claire could see Drew standing in front of the oversize trail map, studying it intently. "She can be a pain—I mean, did you hear her going ballistic before you came upstairs?—but maybe if we take her out a couple times, get her to loosen up, she'll be easier to live with the rest of the summer."

"I don't think she's a pain." So far, Seneca was the one who tested her patience. Drew had been dead-on about Seneca's tendency to steal whatever space she could get.

"She's got a nasty streak, trust me." Seneca sighed, then tightened the towel on her head to keep it from toppling off. "But something's going on at home with her. She seemed really weird when I mentioned her parents. I just got this vibe."

"Vibe?"

Seneca explained that there were messages on the machine—a machine Claire hadn't known they had—and that Drew came in and yelled at her for listening to them. "She can't stand me now—she totally thought I was spying on her—but maybe you can talk to her and get her over whatever's going on. She seems to like you well enough so far."

"I'll try. Problems with parents are something I totally get." Score a surprise point for Seneca for caring about *why* Drew was grumpy.

Maybe she'd judged Miss Hoity-Toity too harshly. Seneca might've grabbed the best of everything in their small bedroom for herself, but she wouldn't be concerned about Drew if she were totally heartless.

Her interest in Aaron could be a way to make nice, too. Not an interest in Aaron for the usual reasons girls were interested in Aaron. Seneca hadn't seen him yet; she couldn't know a thing about him other than his name, which she'd learned thanks to Amanda and Delia.

Sorry, God. I shouldn't make assumptions. I know you have me rooming with them for a reason.

Just last night she'd read the passages in her new Bible about a time and season for every purpose under heaven. They were all she could manage before shutting off the light, anxious to get some sleep before moving into the cabin and spending her first day at King's Crown. It couldn't be coincidence.

I just need to learn to put my trust in you, God. To do it as wholeheartedly as Drew goes after her running.

"Thanks." Seneca gestured toward her bed, which was covered with what had to be every product ever sold by Sephora. "I'll clean this up while you're getting ready. But I'll need to get back in there in ten or fifteen minutes to wash the goop off my face."

"No problem, as long as I can have the mirror to do my makeup when you're done." She could blow her hair dry in the bedroom while Seneca degooped.

Exactly twenty-nine minutes later, Claire bolted out the cabin door. As soon as she got in the car, she blasted the air-conditioning, hoping it'd keep her from getting too disgusting and maybe help finish drying her hair. The air outside was getting thick; it'd probably rain overnight. The sun was still up and she couldn't see any clouds threatening as she drove down the mountain, but that would change soon. In the meantime Aaron was probably going to see her with frizzy hair.

She managed to wiggle the car into a parallel spot on a quiet side street less than a block from the restaurant where she'd first met Aaron last summer. He'd seen her eating at a corner table with her parents, then headed for the rest rooms at the same time she did, just so he could make eye contact and find out her name.

Not only did he find out her name, he'd told her she was the most gorgeous girl he'd seen in weeks. When she told her friends about it, it sounded silly. But in reality he'd done it in a crazy, compelling way that made her think, *I want this guy.*

When she'd bumped into him at a downtown pizza parlor two days later, they'd had instant chemistry—they were kissing within the hour—and he admitted that after that night in the restaurant, he'd asked around until he learned who her friends were and which places in town were her favorites.

He'd hit them all until he found her again.

She stepped out of the car, punched the lock button, then hooked her purse over her shoulder. Maybe eating here tonight would remind him how intensely he loved her.

"You look in-freakin'-credible."

Claire jumped as hands caught her waist from

behind. Aaron's arms—strong and tan, with a dusting of the lightest blond hair—wrapped around her, and then his mouth was at her ear. "I saw you drive by and jogged down the street to meet you. Couldn't wait. And I love the new haircut. Did you get highlights or something?"

"Very observant." She'd wondered as she sat in the beauty salon with foils in her hair and the acid smell giving her a headache if he'd notice the effort. Should've known that he would. He always noticed things like that.

She pushed the car door shut, then spun in his arms. Was it her imagination or had he gotten a little taller since spring break? "I missed—"

His mouth was over hers before she could finish. She closed her eyes, allowing herself to enjoy it. Man, could he kiss. She reached up, feeling the firmness of his chest, the line of his jaw, the softness of his hair. His hair was longer than the last time she'd seen him. A little wilder. She could actually get her fingers into it.

While one hand stayed at the back of his head, she let her other drop down to his waist. She pulled him closer, then opened her mouth a little wider, let him kiss her harder.

He tasted and smelled like California. Shampoo and warmth. Sunshine and energy.

He walked her back a step so her rear was against the

side of the Lexus. His hips fit right against hers, just like she remembered.

Why couldn't they have lived, like, a couple hundred years ago? They'd be married at sixteen or seventeen. They'd have their own place where they could make love whenever they wanted and people would actually think it was a *good* thing.

She wouldn't worry about getting pregnant.

She wouldn't worry about something that felt so absolutely right being a sin; God would be on her side if she wanted to sleep with her husband.

She eased back. Still nose to nose, she whispered, "I take it your flight was okay?"

He laughed. "Yeah. Not fast enough, though." He kissed her forehead, then pulled her into a tight, reassuring hug. "I missed you so much, you have no idea. IM's and phone calls aren't the same."

"No, they're not." Had that come out sounding a little strange? Had she said it in a way that would make him suspect she'd been keeping things from him?

"We have dinner reservations," he mumbled into her ear. "I shoulda made hotel reservations."

Claire's jaw clenched, but she took a deep breath, telling herself to just relax in his arms and enjoy the moment. "I have to work tomorrow."

"We wouldn't need it all night." He turned his head, dropping a quick kiss on her cheek. "But you're right. We shouldn't stay out too late."

He stepped back, letting her push off from the car, but wrapped an arm around her for the walk to the restaurant. "I saw Todd Mirelli while I was waiting for you," he said as they crossed the street. "His parents sent him into town to grab something from the grocery store, it looked like. He told me he hasn't seen you much this spring. You not hanging out with him anymore?"

"Not on purpose. I've just been busy." And trying to keep out of trouble. Todd was the one local kid—other than her, now that she was going out with Aaron—who was keyed into the holiday crowd from L.A., and who'd hit the bars and dance clubs as hard as she had over the last year.

"I figured." Aaron let go of her, allowing her to walk in front of him as another couple passed them on the sidewalk. When he caught up again he said, "Todd said he's going to The Shed tonight. Invited us to come over after we eat. He knows the bouncer, so we won't have any trouble getting in without ID."

Claire tried to change the subject as they rounded the corner onto the main drag and approached the restaurant, asking Aaron if he'd looked at the menu posted in the window.

He stopped walking and grabbed her hand, forcing her to stop, too.

"You sure you don't have a problem with Todd?"

"No, he's a great guy."

Aaron pulled her closer to the wall, out of the flow of traffic on the sidewalk. He squinted in the late-day sunshine, his clear, light blue eyes seeing more than she was ready to reveal.

"What's up, then? Something."

"I just . . ." Now was her opening. Use it or lose it. "I just had a hard spring. I need to take a break from that crowd. You know how it goes sometimes."

His fingers tightened around hers. "You didn't tell me that. Is it because of spring break, when I was here? We did get pretty plowed. Did we do something to piss people off? Start rumors of some kind?"

"It's not that, really." How to explain that it wasn't a rumor that was the problem but reality?

Aaron frowned in concern. "Todd said you've been going to Teen-whatever-it-is with all the Jesus freaks. Is that true? What would make you do that?"

It was so much harder telling him in person than it had been when she'd practiced this moment in her head. Probably because it wasn't going according to plan. They hadn't made it into the restaurant yet and he'd already figured out something was wrong without her having to tell him. She hadn't counted on that.

His hand came up to cup her cheek. "Claire, you know you can tell me anything. I love you like mad. We're not going inside until you tell me what's going on."

*** NINE ***

Claire glanced up and down the sidewalk. People of all ages—little kids with their parents, wealthy vacationers checking out the shops, teens wanting to be part of the scene—all seemed to be staring at her. She looked back at Aaron. "I don't want to have this conversation here."

Without a word he pulled her back around the corner, onto the side street where she'd parked her car. She followed him to a covered bus stop, where he took a seat on the bench in front of an oversize Chanel ad and patted the space beside him. "Better?"

She sat, leaning back against the face of the too-skinny, black-clad supermodel touting No. 5.

She couldn't get into this. She might've had months to think about what to say, but it had to be perfect. And she didn't have "perfect" nailed quite yet.

That's what dinner was supposed to be for.

"I'm sorry, Aaron. Didn't mean to go all drama queen

on you back there. It wasn't anything." She forced a laugh, hoping to get him to believe she was simply getting emotional from seeing him again after so many months. "You know, we should go eat. We don't want to lose our reservation. It's really not—"

"Don't tell me it's not important. I can see that it is." He looked past Claire, scanning the sidewalk, then right into her eyes. "We're alone. No one else can hear a word you say. Whatever it is, I can help you deal. Okay?"

Claire nodded, then reached out to wrap her fingers around Aaron's. Maybe this would be all right. After all, they loved each other. They trusted each other. They never would have lasted this long otherwise. "We had a lot of fun over spring break."

His voice was low as he answered. "Yeah, we did. It was fun, but special, too."

"I know. But, well, it was probably more *fun* than we should have had." She forced her gaze from their intertwined fingers up to his face. "Aaron, I got pregnant."

His hand twitched in hers. "You—"

"Got pregnant."

His jaw went slack for a second as he struggled to take it in. After a moment of silence he said, "Why didn't you tell me? You have to be three months, almost *four* months . . ."

His gaze dropped to her belly.

"I tried to tell you, I *wanted* to tell you, but it never seemed right to do on the phone or in an IM." She forced herself not to chew her lip. "And I'm not anymore."

His eyes met hers again. "Oh, Claire, you didn't have to—"

"It wasn't an abortion. I miscarried."

"I wasn't going to say that." But his voice held a trace of guilt as he added, "I was going to say that you didn't have to go through that alone."

He pulled her close so Claire could tuck her head under his chin and wrap her arms around his waist. She could feel her eyes welling up, her throat getting tight, her nose tingling. But she couldn't cry. Not until she got the story out. The *whole* story.

"I don't understand," Aaron said. "I mean, we were careful."

"We were also drunk," Claire mumbled into his shirt. He smelled so good. Felt so good. But also so, so wrong. She lifted her head from his chest, forcing herself to face him. She'd gotten this much out; now she had to deal with the rest.

"You think the condom came off? I don't remember anything like that happening." He played with a lock of her hair, which was still damp. His grin was mischievous as he added, "That'd be something I'd remember."

"As I said, we were pretty drunk. On at least one of the occasions over spring break where we had sex, anyway. And even so, accidents happen." Did he think she was lying or something? No, she decided, she could tell from his reaction that he believed her. But the pregnancy didn't seem to faze him as much as she'd expected it would.

"Are you okay now?" he asked. "I mean, health-wise?"

"I'm fine."

Creases lined his forehead. "I'm sorry, hon. I can't believe you went through all that alone. If anything like that happens again—"

"Well, that's the thing. It can't. I don't think I could deal."

She waited. He just looked at her. Didn't say a word, just . . . *looked*.

Finally he shrugged. "Of course it won't happen again. We'll be extra careful. Maybe we should go to a clinic, see if we can get you a prescription for the Pill. Your parents wouldn't have to know, but that way we'll be doubled up on protection and—"

"Aaron." She put a finger over his lips. He couldn't say another word, not *one*, until she spelled it out for him. "I mean, *it can't happen again*. I love you—you know that—but I think God was trying to tell me that having sex when I can't deal with the consequences is wrong. Like

He's giving me a second chance here. I can't blow it."

She let her hand fall to her lap but didn't allow her gaze to waver. And she didn't like what she saw in his eyes. Disbelief. A hint that he thought she might be kidding about God being involved in what happened. Then the realization that she wasn't kidding at all.

A muscle twitched in his jaw. "Just how much time did you spend with the Jesus freaks to get you to feel this way? Was this your parents' idea? You didn't tell them, did you? 'Cause you know what we have, Claire. You know how incredible it is with us. It's not just sex. I'm in love with you. And I know you're in love with me!"

Something inside her cringed as he said "Jesus freaks." So far the kids at Teen Jam weren't her favorite people, but they weren't freaks. And since she believed the same things they did, was Aaron essentially calling her a Jesus freak, too? What was he going to say when she told him she was hoping to go to Mexico with Teen Jam over Thanksgiving?

"I do love you, Aaron. And it wasn't my parents' idea or anyone else's. No one even knows I was pregnant. I didn't tell anyone. I went to Teen Jam a couple times, but the kids there wouldn't even talk to me. I went for *me*. Because I felt like God was trying to tell me to shape up my life before I ruined it and I wanted to find out more. And you know what? I'm going to go again."

"Claire—"

"Don't you realize I could be five months away from being someone's *mother* right now? Don't you understand how that would have changed my life? My relationships with you, my parents—I mean, think of how it might have affected my dad's store, since it's so word-of-mouth around here—not to mention my plans for college. I would have to beg my mom to babysit just so I could finish high school next year!"

Aaron let out a long sigh. "Claire, I do get it. Really. We dodged a bullet—both of us, because it would have been my kid, too—but I think we need to consider ourselves lucky and just be more careful in the future. We can't overreact."

"But—"

He shook his head to silence her, then stood, pulling her up off the bench. The street was still empty, but the sun was setting, shooting streaks of orange and purple through the sky over the King's Crown range off to the west. Sunset usually meant the streets came alive with teens and twenty-somethings, out to see and be seen. They wouldn't have any privacy, even here on the side street, for much longer.

"I know you were overwhelmed, Claire. That you're

still probably overwhelmed by what's gone down. I'm overwhelmed, too, 'cause this is hitting me outta left field, you know? But you can't let an accident completely change who you are. So let's just take this one step at a time, all right? In the meantime, I'll respect your wishes. I won't like it, but if time out from sex is what you want . . ."

"It is." He looked so sweet, so sympathetic. Like he wanted to get her through this and see her to the other side.

He pulled her in for a quick hug, then kissed her forehead, letting his lips linger against her skin. "All right," he whispered. "We'll do it your way."

"Thanks." Never in her life had she felt so relieved. He was mad—even though he wasn't *acting* mad, she could tell he was biting his tongue because he believed she'd change her mind—but she hadn't exactly expected him to cheer about her decision not to sleep with him anymore, either. So for now, she'd take what she could get.

No way did she want to push the argument and risk losing him. He'd always understood her better than her friends at school, better than her parents. In time maybe he'd come all the way around to her point of view.

Thank you, God, for not having him dump me in the meantime.

"Maybe we can still get our dinner reservation," she said, pulling back just far enough to see his face. His eyes looked magical with the light of the sunset reflected in them. How could he be so phenomenal-looking? How lucky could she be that he was all hers for the rest of the summer? That he loved *her* and not one of the zillion Seneca types that flocked to Juniper in the summertime or during Christmas and spring break? "Might be worth a try."

"No way we're getting in now." He laughed. "You know how many people got into town yesterday and today? And they're all going out to eat tonight. No big deal, though. We can just go to The Shed, meet Todd and whoever else is there, and order bar food. You don't mind, do you? It's not steak, but—"

"I'd rather not go to The Shed." She wrinkled her nose. "Not tonight, please? I don't know if you saw it on your way from the airport, but there's a Subway that just opened across the street from the Exxon station on Camarillo Street. We could drive over, grab a sandwich, then find a place to eat outdoors, have some quiet time to ourselves."

Aaron took a step back. "You don't want to go to The Shed? *You?*"

"Look, I'd just rather—"

He held up his hands, palms out flat toward her as if pushing her away. "Claire, come *on*! First you tell me that you don't want to sleep with me, and now you don't want to go out partying with me, either? But no problem, we can just go sit outside somewhere and eat subs and, you know, have *quiet time*? If I have quiet time with you, I'm gonna want to screw you, hon. And *that* is the God's honest truth."

In that instant Claire's world crumbled. "Aaron, *please*. That's not what I'm saying." Though, really, it was. She couldn't party with him anymore. If he'd just trust her, do what she wanted for a couple weeks, he'd realize that it was far better not to spend their summer moving in a haze from one bar or house party to the next. They'd connect on a deeper level and have more fun if they did it her way. "Let's just not go to The Shed tonight, okay?"

His eyes turned hard. "Do you—or do you not—want to spend the summer with me?"

"Of course I do!"

"But not at The Shed. And I bet not at The Final Run or Tabby's or any of the other places we hang out. Not over at Todd Mirelli's, watching movies and drinking beer in the basement, either."

How could she possibly explain this to him? She

ignored his angry stance and moved closer, lifting a strand of his white-blond hair back from his face. "I love you, and it's not that I don't want to do those things, but I don't trust myself. I need to know that I can be out with you and not get drunk and not have sex, and that we can still be a couple and have fun. I need to not screw things up as badly as I did over spring break, Aaron. I need to know that I can get through my senior year and go to college and get a job without getting pregnant or doing something stupid like getting crazy drunk in public again."

Aaron closed his eyes and put his hands on his hips. His chin dipped down against his chest.

"Aaron, please! Say something."

"I can't do this, Claire. I can't."

No, God, no! "Can't do what?"

"I think you know." He opened his eyes but didn't meet her gaze. "I know you've been through about the most intense thing a girl can go through. I get that. But I can't completely change who I am because you suddenly think God is talking to you like you're Joan of Arc or something. So you take your time, you do whatever it is you think God is telling you to do, and you call me when you're all done."

"Aaron, that's not fair!"

"It's not fair to me, either."

She put a hand on his elbow, but he shook her off. "See ya around, Claire. You know where to find me."

He turned and walked away, disappearing into the crowd of shoppers and sightseers without another word.

Claire stood there, stunned. He'd come back. He'd get halfway down the street, pass their restaurant, realize how much he loved her, and he'd come back.

Wouldn't he?

Ten minutes later she was still standing at the bus stop alone. More alone, even, than the day after she'd miscarried, when she'd sat on the bench at Ritter Park wondering what to do with her life.

There had to be something more valuable than sitting around the bars and restaurants of Juniper getting loaded. Why couldn't Aaron see that? Or at least *try* to see that?

She walked to her Lexus, slid into the driver's seat, and flipped open her cell phone. She dialed directory assistance and got the number for the minister who ran Teen Jam.

On the third ring there was a click, then he picked up. His hello nearly did her in. He sounded so warm and friendly, it made her feel like she wasn't alone anymore, just with that one word.

"This is Claire Watts. I don't know if you remember me—"

"Of course I do, Claire. It's great to hear from you."

He sounded like he meant it. "I hope I'm not calling you at a bad time or anything, but I was wondering if it's still possible to volunteer for the Mexico trip. I'll need to talk to my parents, but I can do whatever you need to help with the fund-raising—"

"Of course, Claire. I was hoping you'd sign up. Could you help with the car wash next week?"

"Can I check my work schedule and let you know?"

He told her that was fine, then urged her to swing by the church to pick up an information sheet from his office and to share it with her parents. "I'm impressed that you're willing to give up your school vacation to help, Claire. It's going to be hard work, but I think you'll find it rewarding."

"I do, too," she answered, then thanked him before hanging up.

She dropped the cell phone back into her purse, then looked in the rearview mirror. Behind her, the main drag was getting more and more crowded. But still no sign of Aaron.

Reluctantly, she put the car into drive and headed for Ritter Park. She couldn't go back to the cabin for at least two or three hours—Seneca would have too many questions about why Claire had come back early—and she certainly didn't want to go to her parents' house. They knew Aaron was due in town today, too.

She circled the park twice before finding an end spot, away from the busy playground and the flower gardens that bordered downtown, where she was unlikely to be spotted. She cut the engine and clicked the button to lock the doors, just in case there were whackjobs around.

A squirrel ran under a picnic table near the edge of the lot, picking at the ground for food before disappearing behind a stand of Douglas fir. Claire watched for a moment, willing the squirrel to come back out and distract her. No luck.

She folded her hands, then dropped her head against the steering wheel. It'd probably found its family or a cozy place to snuggle in for the evening. Safe and warm and loved.

God? It's me again. I know this is your plan. . . .

She raised her head and punched the steering wheel. It *had* to be God's plan, didn't it? So why did it have to hurt so much?

✳✳✳ Ten ✳✳✳

Seneca edged sideways through the mass of bodies dancing at The Shed, wondering how it could be that the fire marshal wasn't on scene threatening to issue a fine to the owners for the higher-than-capacity crowd.

She wished they would. These places were always better when they weren't so packed.

After dodging a knot of college-aged girls at the edge of the dance floor—clearly first-timers, since they were oohing and aahing over the selection of shots a waitress brought to them—Seneca approached a large curtained-off area near the rear of the bar. A bald guy in his mid-twenties sat on a stool near the curtain, scanning the crowd.

"Hey, Mikey. Got space for your favorite girl in there?"

The bald guy instantly perked up. "Seneca, baby! Haven't seen you in a while. Heard you weren't in town anymore."

She moved a half step closer and grinned. "Can't always believe what you hear."

"Twenty-one and up to get in. Got ID?"

"Of course." She flashed her fake ID. Mikey barely gave it a glance.

"It's tight in there, but I can let you in." He eased the thick blue velvet curtain aside to reveal a pair of black doors, then pushed one open for her.

She gave him a smile but paused before entering. "Violet and Dahlia around?"

"Haven't seen 'em yet."

Fantastic. She thanked him, then ducked into the private lounge. Mikey was right. There were more people in here than usual, though it remained far quieter than out in the main bar area. No one was dancing; no one was spilling beer on the floor. Rather, comfy banquettes lined the walls, all filled with what she considered the in crowd of college kids, most of whom were from southern California or New York. A few high schoolers were in the mix. Music emanated from hidden speakers. Most groups were deep in conversation, sipping drinks as they traded stories about what they'd done since they'd last seen each other in Juniper.

Todd Mirelli was standing at the bar laughing with a good-looking blond guy she didn't recognize. He had to be *someone* or Todd wouldn't be hanging with him. From their appearance—shirts hanging loose, goofy grins—she guessed the beers they were holding weren't their first.

She glanced at her watch. It was after nine, so they'd probably been here a while. Maybe they'd be chatty and she could figure out what dirt the Koss sisters were spreading about her. Had they told Todd it was her phone they'd tossed out of the car? Did they tell him she was working at King's Crown?

If things went well, she could introduce herself to Todd's friend and see if it was worth making him her friend, too.

"Hey, Seneca!"

She turned in the direction of the male voice. A burly guy in a Princeton T-shirt and jeans was grinning and waving her to the table he shared with a half-dozen others. She couldn't remember his name but his face was vaguely familiar. Judging from the assortment of designer purses tucked under the table and the girls' shoes, he was with the money crowd. She must've met him somewhere last summer, since she didn't recall seeing him at Mr. Koss's birthday bash.

She smiled back, making certain it was perky enough to be flirty but not so much that she appeared relieved to see a familiar face, then slowly made her way to his table.

Good thing she'd decided to come out tonight. After Claire left there'd been no sense in hanging out at the cabin—not alone with Drew anyway—so she'd pulled on a spaghetti-strapped pink Vivienne Tam dress that showed off her shoulders and finagled a ride to The Shed, hoping it'd be worth the effort.

Now, at the very least, she had a ride home. At the best, a new group of friends.

She air-kissed Princeton Guy. "Hey, great to see you!" Though he was impossibly average-looking, she added, "You look amazing, as always."

"You too, Seneca. I don't think I've seen you since, what? I guess that party at your mom and Axel's place last June."

"Yep, that's it. It's been forever!" Now she remembered. Not his name, but where she'd seen him. His mom was the CEO of a luxury hotel chain and had a house less than a mile from Axel's. Rumor had it that Axel's dogs got out during the party and pooped next to her pool.

What in the world was his *name*?

Without being asked, a hand-holding couple sitting at the edge of the banquette scooted in farther so Seneca could join Princeton Guy. She thanked them but stayed standing.

"Want me to go order some more drinks first? You guys look like you need refills."

When they all nodded and started calling out orders, Seneca glanced at Princeton. "Gotta pen? Let's write all these down."

He looked to each person in turn and wrote their names and drinks on a napkin. Then he scribbled *Adam—Rolling Rock* at the bottom and said, "If they don't have Rolling Rock, can you order me a Bass?"

"Will do." That was it—Adam Blaylock! And now she had a cheat sheet with everyone else's names in case she needed to remember certain people later.

"You need help carrying?"

She shook her head. "They'll bring it over. Back in a sec."

Seneca smiled to herself as she walked to the bar. This could be a very productive night. She read the order off to the bartender. As she'd predicted, he offered to bring everything to the table when it was ready. She was about to turn back to the table when she heard Todd Mirelli's voice.

"That's just wrong," he was saying. His words were slurred and difficult to understand but Seneca got the impression a heavy conversation was taking place between Todd and his friend. Especially when Todd added, "She's not the type to pull that kind of crap. You sure you're tellin' me everything? She must've had a reason. She loves you, man."

Seneca reached for one of the bar menus and pretended to read while she listened in.

The blond guy started to say something in response, but Seneca couldn't make out the words. Then she clearly heard him ask Todd, "You okay, dude? You look like you're gonna be sick."

She sneaked a peek over the menu in time to see Todd nod that he was okay, then barf right into his beer glass. It spilled over onto the bar and a half-eaten plate of quesadillas, pooling against the bar's edge. The blond guy looked ready to bolt at the sight.

The bartender grabbed a towel and shouted for Mikey. He threw the towel in front of Todd. "What the hell, Mirelli?"

The only response the bartender got was another loud retch. Two girls standing nearby wrinkled their noses and moved away, then pointed out Todd to a group of well-dressed teens at a nearby table.

Seneca set down the menu and turned away with a shudder as the bartender yelled for Mikey again.

So much for hearing gossip. Or for meeting whoever the cutie blond guy was with Todd. Those two would be lucky if Mikey let them back in the lounge for the rest of the summer. Especially Todd, since he was underage. If he went home like that and the police stopped him The Shed could lose its liquor license.

She returned to the table, where one of the girls, an exotic-looking brunette with impossibly golden skin named Gabriela, was talking about starting an internship at the Creative Artists Agency in a couple weeks.

"CAA?" a guy down the table said. "My brother's an agent there. I'll give him a call and make sure you're all set." After Gabriela thanked him, the guy glanced at Seneca. "Your mom repped by CAA?"

"No, but a number of her friends are."

Seneca's mood brightened, despite the fact that Adam had casually draped his arm on the banquette behind her. Whatever. Adam wasn't her type, but it wouldn't hurt to hang out here and be his friend for the evening, especially if it got her a solid contact at CAA.

A few minutes later the bartender brought over their drinks. As Seneca thanked him for her tonic water with lime—a drink that would allow her to keep a clear head but make everyone else at the table think she was having her trademark Grey Goose and tonic—she noticed Mikey hefting a very drunk Todd Mirelli by the armpits, half dragging, half walking him toward the bathroom. The blond guy who'd been telling Todd about his girl trouble was nowhere in sight.

Adam's arm slipped from the banquette onto Seneca's shoulders. She took a sip of her tonic water, trying to ignore the creeping feeling in her gut that warned her to get out of there before Adam got any ideas.

She *had* to do this. This was the right crowd. The L.A. crowd. It was where she belonged.

Of course, that was probably what Mom thought about Axel, even after he started being an ass and demanding that she cut her work schedule. That she *belonged* with a power player like him.

Seneca leaned forward and chatted up Gabriela and the guy with the talent-agent brother for a while. She even managed to drop a hint that her mom might be in the market for a new agent. When the subject drifted to college applications, Seneca feigned interest and discreetly slid her hand into her purse and held down a button on her phone. A minute later, just as Adam started moving his fingers along her shoulder in a slow caress (did he think he was being subtle?), Seneca's phone rang.

She pulled it from her purse, answered the call, and listened. Thank God she'd read about that callback service and preprogrammed it into her phone. She furrowed her brow, then made a few concerned-sounding "Are you kidding me?" and "I'm sure it'll be fine" comments. She finished with a determined "I'll be right there" and flipped the phone shut.

"Trouble?" Adam asked.

"Nothing too serious," she said, keeping her voice light but making sure she kept a semiworried expression on her face, so he'd think she had an emergency she needed to keep to herself. "But I have to go. I'm so sorry. I'll catch you soon, okay, Adam?"

"Sure." He asked for her cell number to call her later.

She was about to dodge, but then Gabriela asked if she could have it, too. Seneca smiled and gave it to both of them before hustling out the door.

Not her best night so far, given that she'd have to find a way to politely avoid Adam's call, but it was definitely progress.

And it was still early enough to hit another bar.

✳✳✳ Eleven ✳✳✳

Drew knew the phone would ring, and that it would ring damned early in the morning. It might be only their third week of summer employment at King's Crown, but there was a 100 percent guarantee that on her days off the entire cabin would be awakened by the ringing telephone, and Drew would be forced to listen to her mother's I-miss-you-but-I-know-this-is-best whining.

She could strangle Marla for mailing work schedules out to all the summer employees' parents. Wasn't that an invasion of privacy or something? Did parents *really* need to know when they were supposed to be calling or visiting and when they weren't?

Of course, Mom would be calling today whether she knew Drew's schedule or not. It was the anniversary of the worst day in her entire friggin' life. Mom probably had it marked in red on the calendar.

Drew rolled over to look at the glowing digital numbers

on her bedside clock. Six thirty. Why in the world was she awake now? Normally she was *not* a morning person. Even on days when she had school or an important track meet she hated being disturbed before seven thirty. It wasn't natural. So what if she showed up to class with wet hair?

She flipped back over, grabbing her pillow and mushing it so it'd do a better job supporting her head and neck. She was going to have to ask one of the lodge's cleaning ladies if they could grab her another from supply. This one sucked.

"Drew? You awake?"

Claire. Probably what woke her up. The girl never seemed to sleep; she just sat downstairs staring at the television half the night and lay awake in bed the other half. When Drew met Claire that first day—and even before that, when she'd eavesdropped on Claire's conversation during orientation—she'd gotten the impression Claire was a typical sixteen- or seventeen-year-old. Worried about what people like those Amanda and Delia chicks thought of her, yeah. But still *normal*.

Since then, however, Drew had started to wonder if Claire needed to get herself medicated. Claire's moodiness and her TV habits reminded Drew a little too much of her own mother's behavior.

S-c-a-r-y.

"Drew?" Claire whispered again.

"Yeah, I'm awake," Drew muttered.

"Um, your mother called last night while you were running with Rob. Forgot to tell you. She said for you to call her first thing this morning."

"Thanks, Claire. I'll call her in a couple hours."

"Oh. Okay."

After a few minutes Drew heard Claire get up, ruffle through the stack of beauty and fitness magazines that had accumulated on their bedroom floor, then tiptoe downstairs.

An hour later, Drew still hadn't gotten back to sleep. The smell of Claire making coffee in their cheapo coffeemaker didn't help. She threw back the sheets, pulled on a pair of running shorts and a sports bra, then grabbed a ponytail holder from the nightstand and a thin running shirt from her drawer. She glanced in the direction of Seneca's bed to make sure Miss Hollywood had gotten home from her night out. Upon seeing the appropriate-size lump under the covers and the sprawl of dark hair on the pillow, Drew ambled down the stairs, pulling the shirt over her head as she went.

Sure enough, Claire was sitting on the couch, morning news muted on the television, slurping down a cup of coffee and reading a year-old copy of *Self*.

At least it wasn't her Bible. She always seemed more emotional when huddled up on her bed or the couch with her Bible.

Claire laid the magazine down on her lap. "Want some coffee?"

Drew shook her head as she pulled her hair back into a tight ponytail, one that'd keep loose strands from getting in her face and bugging her. "I think I'm going to go for a run."

The bridge of Claire's nose wrinkled. "Don't you usually go in the evening? With Rob?"

"Yeah, usually." Ever since the third day of work, they'd met at five thirty for a run. She wasn't sure what she liked more, the actual running or the fact she was running with Rob, but she'd grown accustomed to the altitude and knew she was getting faster. So something had to be working. "I'll probably meet him tonight, too."

"You're going twice?"

Drew shrugged. "I can't sleep and it's my day off, so I may as well make use of the time."

"You want to go into town? I mean, since you have the whole day off? You're welcome to borrow my car."

"And do what? Not much to do unless you're willing

to spend money, and I'm not. Thanks for the offer, though."

That elicited a tentative smile from Claire. "Yeah, you don't strike me as the shopping type."

Not at Juniper prices, for sure.

Claire took a long slug of her coffee, then said, "Next time we're both off, want to go for a ride on mountain bikes? I know I haven't mentioned it since that first day we met, but I really did mean it."

Drew told her she'd love it, and Claire brightened. As Drew bent to pull on one of her running shoes Claire looked back down at the magazine, which Drew noticed was open to an article titled "Ten Ways to Boost Your Self-Confidence." But it was obvious to Drew that Claire wasn't seeing the words on the page.

"Hey, Claire"—she glanced in the direction of the staircase to be sure Seneca was asleep, then continued in a low voice— "is something going on with you? You haven't mentioned Aaron once since our first day, even though I've heard Seneca ask you about him a few times."

Drew yanked on her second running shoe, hoping Claire would take it as a sign that she was willing to listen if she needed a friend, but that she wouldn't butt in or be offended if Claire wasn't up to talking.

"Seneca asks a lot of questions about *everything*,"

Claire replied in a quiet voice, rolling her eyes. "I think she's going through a tough time, though, so I just let her questions go."

"Seneca?" Little Miss Hollywood, who managed to drop "My mommy has an Oscar" into at least three conversations in the last week? Please. "What on Earth makes you think *that*?"

"I saw her in the Business Center the other morning on my way to work. She was sitting at one of the computers and looked really serious. Worried. I watched her through the glass doors for a little bit, then popped my head in. She got all cheery when she saw me and said she was just IM-ing her mom before starting her shift in the spa. I got the feeling they were discussing something heavy."

Drew tried not to look skeptical. "Heavy" to Seneca probably meant her mom was a day late sending her a check. "I'm sure Seneca will work it out." A little more money from her mother, maybe a new bottle of facial muck, and she'd be happy again.

"You're changing the subject, you know," Drew told Claire. "I asked how *you* were doing, not Seneca. But that's cool if you want to keep it—"

"Aaron and I broke up."

Figured. Why did girls get so hung up on guys who weren't worth it? Let themselves fall into a funk that wouldn't help a damned thing? "I'm sorry, Claire."

"Me too." Claire shifted on the sofa. "Look, can you not tell Delia or Amanda if they say anything to you? And not Seneca, either. I don't want her to know."

"Why would I? I never see Amanda and Delia anyway, since they go home when their shifts end." And Seneca . . . Drew had heard Seneca ask Claire last week about when Aaron might come by their cabin to meet everyone. When Claire shrugged and wanted to know why she was so curious, Seneca mentioned that his parents had been in the spa and that's why she was asking. Seneca also mentioned something about how Aaron's dad headed a production company. Seneca had practically salivated over the phrase "production company."

Drew frowned at Claire. "You think Seneca's after Aaron?"

"I don't know," Claire said after another sip of coffee. "Maybe. But I'd rather not discuss it with her either way. You're the only person I've told."

After three weeks? Seemed like a long time for Claire to keep it bottled up. "You gonna be okay?"

Claire shrugged. "Not much choice. But I don't feel the same without him. It's like part of me is missing and I can't get it back."

"Well, I know it feels awful now, but . . ." Drew hesitated, hoping her words wouldn't come out wrong. "Try to think ahead to how you're going to feel in a few months. You're probably upset because you liked him, yeah, but the bigger reason is because you started to depend on him. And after a few months on your own—and a few more magazine articles about building self-confidence—you'll realize that you're better off because you've learned not to depend on a guy. *Any* guy."

Claire straightened on the sofa. Still keeping her voice low, presumably so Seneca wouldn't wake up, she replied, "You get stomped on by a guy you depended on?"

"No, but I watched it happen to my mom. Not pretty . . ." Drew let her words drift off. She hadn't meant to say quite so much. But maybe it'd help Claire snap out of her funk. No way could Aaron be worth all the sniffly crybaby depression Claire was enduring.

What was it with girls defining themselves by what a solitary member of the male species thought of them?

"You've never said much about your parents, Drew. Are they divor—"

"No, no divorce." And no way she wanted to say anything more than that.

Claire frowned. "That first day, when you and Seneca argued upstairs, she told me that you had a phone call from your mom. She got the impression things were rough at home for you, too. Something you want to talk about?"

The phone rang, cutting through their conversation. Speak of the devil. But for once Mom's timing was good. Drew stepped past Claire and grabbed the handset on the second ring. "Hello?"

"Oh, I'm so glad you're there. I was afraid I'd get that answering machine again."

"Hi, Mom. You're calling early." Drew rolled her eyes at Claire. Claire gave her an understanding look, then stood up and took her magazine outside.

Drew had to give her props for being considerate. Seneca would've taken a few steps away, just to give the appearance she wanted Drew to have privacy, then strained to hear all she could. And given the fact she'd apparently blabbed immediately to Claire about the phone message that first day, Seneca would probably blab about it to anyone who cared to listen.

"If I don't call early, you're not there," her mother replied with only a modest amount of accusation in her voice. She was probably saving up for something more important. "Is everything going well? Did you have a good week? It's your day off today, right?"

"Yes, yes, and yes, Mom. I'm fine." She listened for Seneca, wondering if the phone's ring awakened her, but didn't hear anything. And Seneca wasn't exactly stealthy. Keeping her voice down, Drew said, "I think you need to worry more about yourself. Did you make an appointment with the therapist the Army doc recommended?"

"Oh, they're just going to tell me I'm depressed and want to give me drugs. I don't need drugs. Drugs won't change what happened." With forced liveliness she added, "I'm doing better, though. So don't worry."

Right. "How are you doing better, Mom?"

"I went to your dad's grave and talked to him last night. I know you think that's silly, but it feels good to talk to him. I told him it's been a year, and that we still miss him."

Drew sat on the couch and covered her forehead with one hand. If Dad were able, he'd step right outta that grave and kick Mom's ass. Tell her to freaking *get a life* and stop spending every single moment wishing for him to come back.

He wasn't coming back.

"Mom, have you thought about moving back home?"

"Oh, honey, we've had this conversation before. I *am* home."

"Leavenworth isn't home. It's just a post where Dad got stationed. If he were alive, we wouldn't even be living there anymore. We'd be on to his next assignment. And it's not like you're even in the house where we lived on post. Even the Army is trying to tell you that Leavenworth isn't your home!"

"Drew, you're crossing that line we talked about."

True, but pushing Mom was easier when they weren't face to face. And what did she have to lose? "Why don't we move back to West Virginia so you can be near Grandma and Grandpa and Aunt Wendy? You can get a job in a library there, and—"

"For the last time, Drew, I'm not going to West Virginia. First, library jobs aren't as easy to come by as you think. Second, you shouldn't have to change schools right before your senior—"

"I've changed schools eight times since kindergarten. Once more is no big deal." And that was the truth. She would miss her friends, but the high school near Aunt Wendy and her grandparents had a good track team and one of the best cross-country programs in the nation. She'd deal. Having family around would give her mom something else to focus on besides the fact her husband was dead.

Help Mom see that, at forty years old, she still had a life worth living.

"And third," her mom continued as if Drew hadn't spoken, "my parents and Aunt Wendy were never big fans of your father. They thought we got married too young and they were really upset when he joined the Army. So I don't want to be where they can say 'I told you so' or insert themselves into my life on a daily basis. All right?"

"What about Colorado? Aunt Jo's here, and—"

"I'm not going to live near your father's sister, either."

Dumb suggestion. Mom and Aunt Jo used to be real tight, but that was before Dad died. Before Aunt Jo sent the info about the King's Crown job without getting Mom's parental seal of approval first.

"I can understand that." Drew massaged her forehead. "But promise me you'll think a little more about West Virginia, at least?"

How many times had they had this conversation in one form or the other in the last year? Same outcome every time. Mom would make noises about doing what she thought was best, go to work if it was a workday, then come home and refuse to do anything other than half-heartedly flip through TV channels until it was time for Letterman. If she had to, she'd pay a bill or two, but that was it. She wouldn't return calls from the women who'd been their neighbors while they lived on post, or the women who belonged to the Officer's Wives Club or the swimming pool or who enjoyed any of the other stuff Mom had participated in before Dad died.

Life on autopilot. No goals. No drive. No future.

"Drew, this is silly. Let's talk about something else. Have you sent any postcards to your friends yet? A couple of them stopped into the library and told me to tell you hello."

"Mom, they're just making polite conversation. They know how I am. I've e-mailed a few times."

"Well, you should send postcards."

The rest of the conversation was more of the same, with Drew trying to get her mom to *do* something—go to the swimming pool, catch a movie with a neighbor, go golfing with some of her old friends—and her mom turning the conversation back to a variation on getting Drew more excited about living in Leavenworth, telling Drew how much she was missed and how hard it was without her around the house.

Finally, when Mom got to the sobby stage, Drew claimed that her roommates were getting ready for work and it wasn't a good time to talk.

"Drew, we'll be all right, both of us. Here in Leavenworth. It just takes time."

Drew fought not to snap back, *And a healthy dose of therapy for you.* "We'll see. I've gotta go. Bye, Mom."

After replacing the handset, Drew walked to the stairs, heard Seneca's low snoring, and heaved a sigh of relief.

The last thing she needed was to listen to questions from bricks-for-brains.

When Drew stepped outside, Claire was nowhere to be seen. Probably headed up to the lodge for breakfast. Good thing Claire had slept in a pair of shorts and a T-shirt instead of her usual cutesy jammies. The fluffy stuff wouldn't have gone over well in the employee cafeteria.

Drew did a few light stretches, then took off along one of the strenuous trails, skipping the six-mile Aspen Leaf, which she was still dying to do, in favor of a four-miler called Rocky Ridge. If she could conquer Rocky Ridge and get to where she was comfortable running it, she'd be ready to tackle the Aspen Leaf.

Running with Rob the last three weeks had improved her speed and endurance faster than she'd dreamed possible. Plus he was great company. Funny and easy to talk to, yet not nosy about her personal life. Challenging on the running front, but—at least since the footsie episode in the cafeteria—not a threat to her mental state. Not once had he tried to flirt with her since then.

Good thing, too. Mom was all she could deal with on the emotional side of life right now.

As she passed the post marking the start of the trail, Drew reached for her left wrist and clicked the tiny button on the side of her watch to start the timer. According to the trail map, the first part of the run was straight uphill, then it curved around a ridge, took a slight downhill then a short but steep uphill before finishing with a long, gentle downhill cruise back into the lodge area. A nice leg- and butt-burner.

Drew let thoughts of her mother drift away as she ran out of sight of the lodge and took in the views. She'd gotten used to having Rob to talk to and had forgotten to bring her iPod, but decided it didn't matter. Going on a run like this one—alone, with nothing but the fresh air and the tall evergreens surrounding her—might help her clear her head, get some perspective. Do what was best for *her* by getting the adrenaline pumping, reveling in the rush of power that came from tackling a hill, concentrating on the pattern of her own breathing.

Reminding herself that mental strength and physical training could get her through anything.

Maybe she could talk Mom into letting her come out here to college. Get away from Kansas, make a new start for herself in the mountains. She glanced off to the west as she reached the top of the hill, following the trail as it took a long curve around the ridge. Mountaintop after mountaintop filled her view, each peak stretching up to kiss the clouds as far as she could see into the distance. The sun was high enough in the sky now to make each peak glow, but the valleys between the mountains still appeared dark, mysterious.

Like God had laid out the entire vision just for her.

A low, threatening rumble came from somewhere ahead of her. Drew inhaled sharply and jerked up short. A pain shot through her ankle but she ignored it at the sight in front of her.

Bear. Dark. Massive. *Bear*.

✳✳✳ TWELVE ✳✳✳

Drew choked back a wave of puke. The thing was *right there*. Bigger than Drew ever imagined a bear might be, standing on its back legs, rubbing its shoulder against a thick tree trunk at the side of the trail.

The tree creaked from the bear's weight.

No sound left her mouth, though instinct made Drew want to scream.

Stay calm, stay calm!

How many lectures had Hud given them about the possibility of seeing a black bear or mountain lion while out on the trails? He'd said there were things they could do to avoid confrontation or attack.

Drew's heart thudded as she tried to remember Hud's exact words.

Don't make eye contact. Give it lots of room to escape. Try to stand tall so you look large. If you're on a trail, go off the downhill side slowly.

What else? What else?

Back away. Keep facing the bear.

She was not calm. She did *not* want to back away. Everything in her made her want to turn and run for it.

She spread her feet and arms, trying to look larger, like a bigger animal than the bear would want to take on, and took a slow step backward.

When the morning hikers came through and found her mangled body, what would they tell her mom?

Mom wouldn't be able to handle it. She'd fall completely apart.

I'm not ready to die.

She'd be in the ground, next to Dad. Mom would never leave Kansas then. Never leave the friggin' cemetery.

A soft noise came from behind her and Drew's eyes filled with hot tears.

No! How could she face this bear if there was another at her back? She twitched, trying to look in the direction of the sound without losing sight of the bear in front of her.

"Don't turn around. I have a stick."

"Rob?" she whispered.

"Yeah." The bear dropped down to all fours and looked at her. Oh, *no!*

"Stay calm. Don't meet its gaze or it'll think you're challenging it. It's about to move away."

She was going to throw up for real now. Swallowing hard, she muttered, "Not fast enough."

She felt his hand on her lower back. "If it comes at us, clap loudly and yell. I'll whack it with the stick. Fight. They don't like noise."

Fight a bear? No one spent enough hours in the gym to fight something so huge. One halfhearted swipe from that thing and she'd be done.

But Rob was right about the bear moving away. After making a few more grunting noises, it lumbered off the side of the trail and into the trees. As it got farther from the trail it picked up its pace, until it was out of sight in the thick greenery.

"Good job," Rob said. He walked around to face her and put a hand on each of her wrists. "Um, Drew, you can put your arms down now."

"It's not coming back?" She let her arms drop to her sides.

"No, they really don't like humans. They stay away from us when they can. Can't blame 'em." One side of his mouth cocked up into a smile. "Hey, you all right?"

"I will be. Give me a sec. Holy—" she felt her knees start to shake and willed herself to stay upright.

"You did exactly the right thing. I think that's only the

third or fourth time a bear's been seen on one of the resort's trails."

"Leave it to me to find one."

Rob laughed. "You shouldn't be out here alone at sunrise, you know. They like to be out at dusk and dawn."

She pulled her wrists free, stumbled to the edge of the trail, bent over to put her hands on her knees, and vomited so hard she splashed the rocks and weeds.

"Sorry," she mumbled, then vomited again, doing a little backstep to keep from hitting her good running shoes. Of all the people to see her this way. Right after he rescued her, too.

When her stomach was empty, she swiped her mouth with the hem of her running shirt, took a few breaths to stop herself from dry-heaving, then straightened. Why should she care what Rob thought? It wasn't like she was interested in him or anything.

Anyone coming up behind her would have scared away the bear. Maybe *she'd* scared away the bear.

Maybe she was going loony from the shock. Because somewhere inside, she realized she had at least a mild case of shock. And that she needed to hide it from Rob.

He took a step closer to her. "Want a drink? I have my canteen."

"I'm good." Okay, not *good*, but she wasn't going to put her barfo mouth on his canteen knowing he'd have to clean it later.

She might not care what he thought about her in general, but that would just be rude.

"Want me to walk you back to the lodge?"

She shook her head. Bad enough he saw her looking scared. She didn't need the entire staff to see him walk her back like she was a lost child. "I'm halfway already. May as well finish the run." Assuming there weren't any more bears ahead.

"Want company?"

She did, but not if it made her look like some candy-ass chick who needed a guy around simply to function. She studied him, trying to decide, and noticed for the first time that he wasn't dressed in his regular running gear. "You can't run. You're in long shorts and hiking boots."

"I was doing the weekly inspection of the trail when I came up behind you. But no big deal—it's only two miles and mostly downhill from here to the lodge. If you don't sprint I'll be fine. Drew" —he put a hand on her shoulder, though the touch was tentative—"I think you need someone to run with you. You look wrecked."

"I'm fine."

"You're not. You're crying."

"I'm not—"

He took his hand from her shoulder and wiped her cheek, then held up moistened fingertips. "That's not sweat."

"So the bear scared me." Nothing, *nothing* on the planet bugged her more than having someone see her cry. And worse, she hadn't even *realized* she was crying. "And barfing up my guts probably made my eyes water."

"Drew—"

"Oh, *fine*. You can run with me if you want, hiker boy." Better than having him think of her as a girly-girl wimp. She turned to run but sucked in a breath as her ankle threatened to collapse beneath her on the first hard step. Now she remembered.

Damn bear. She'd cocked her ankle sideways trying to stop when she'd seen it.

"You're hurt."

"Nice observation skills there, Sherlock." She tried to say it in a jokey tone, though she felt anything but. She bent down, inspecting her ankle. The inside was puffy at the top of her sock.

Could her day possibly get any worse?

"Can you walk?"

She nodded, but her face flushed hot. Walking was

going to hurt, too. Especially going for two miles, even if most of it was downhill.

This better not screw up her cross-country season.

She took a few steps. Beside her, Rob looked overly concerned. "I dunno."

"Rob, I'm fine."

But she wasn't. And the tears were coming again. *Damn.*

"Let's sit for a sec. Elevate the ankle for a bit, then you can try again." He eased her toward a large rock on the side of the path, a place where they'd have a good view if the bear approached again, then sat beside her.

As he brushed away some dirt from his side of the rock she tried to fake like she was wiping away sweat, but it didn't work. There were too many tears now.

"It's more than the bear, isn't it? And more than the ankle, too."

"Sorry," she gritted out. "I'm not usually such a wuss. It's been a rough morning."

He was silent for a few moments. As much as she didn't want to like the guy, she liked the guy. It was more than just the dark, expressive eyes that made her want to stare at him until she figured him out. More than the fact he was a great runner, or that he did things in his own competent, quiet way. More than the fact that all the other summer employees respected him without him having to demand it. And more than the fact he was quiet now, respecting her privacy.

He possessed that intangible something that made her recognize he could be her soulmate.

The realization scared her almost as much as the bear had.

"Why don't you go ahead?" Drew said. "My ankle is fine. Really, I'd tell you if I needed help. But I think I need some time alone."

His voice low and calm, he said, "I saw Claire in the employee cafeteria this morning, right before I left to walk up here. She mentioned that you were on the phone with your mother and needed some privacy."

Did the guy not hear a word she'd just said?

"I take it the call didn't go so well."

"Nothing new," she replied, looking down at her shoes, trying not to be mad at the swollen ankle. Or at her mom or the bear or at Claire for opening her big mouth.

Crap. This wasn't Claire's fault. It was 100 percent her own.

"Nothing new, but nothing good, huh?"

She shook her head. She couldn't speak.

And then she did.

"It's just . . . my dad was killed in Iraq by a roadside bomb. It happened a year ago today."

Rob's arm came around her back. He didn't say a word, but he didn't have to. Just that touch—the way he was comforting, not grabby—told her what she needed to know.

"He was an Army doctor. A major. These two guys in dress uniforms—they call them casualty assistance calls officers, but I think they should just call them the Death Squad 'cause that's what they really are—they came to the door and the neighbors across the hall . . ."

She paused to snarf up the snot that was filling her nose. "We lived in Pope-Doniphan, which means nothing to you, but they were the best quarters we ever had, with these really high ceilings and columns out front. Anyway, the neighbors heard everything because our quarters shared a front hallway with theirs and Mom collapsed right there on the tile when she saw it was the Death Squad at the door and they had to get an ambulance for her. Then we had to move off post because you can't stay in Army housing if your sponsor is dead so my mom bought this horrid house in Leavenworth instead of going home to West Virginia so she could be near his grave because they buried him at Fort Leavenworth and she still can't function and it's awful and I don't think it's ever going to change. And kids at school—it's the same high school whether you're a civilian or you live on post 'cause they don't have a high school on post—they either feel sorry for me and talk to me in this sad little voice like I'm a kid who fell off her bike or they go 100 percent the other direction and won't even look at me because it reminds them that their dads and moms could die, too, and I'm babbling and I'm sorry, I'm really sorry, because this isn't me. I hate people who whine and who can't just shut up and solve their own problems already instead of dumping them on other people."

She looked sideways at him. In a voice that sounded strangled even to her own ears she said, "I'm sorry. I shouldn't . . . I mean, this isn't—"

"Drew, I know it's not you."

She could see in his face that he didn't mind hearing her babble. He didn't think she was a nut. He wouldn't spread it around or talk about it with Claire or Seneca or anyone else if she didn't want him to.

And he didn't think of her as pathetic. At least not yet.

His arm tightened around her shoulders. She leaned into his shoulder, her forehead resting against his neck.

"Doctors aren't supposed to get killed," she whispered. "That's what he told me before he left. That doctors were relatively safe and that I shouldn't worry about him. He said he'd be careful."

"Drew, no one's supposed to get killed. No one."

"I know. But he did." She wrapped her arms around his waist. It was just for a minute. Just until she got herself under control.

She'd deal with the consequences tomorrow. After she and Rob figured out how to get down the mountain.

She closed her eyes and let him kiss the top of her head.

Maybe she could stay more than a minute.

"Thank you," she whispered into his shoulder.

He didn't say anything. He just held her close and let her cry.

❊❊❊ THIRTEEN ❊❊❊

"So, Seneca Billeray, daughter of highly acclaimed actress Jacqueline Billeray, why don't you give us your insider's opinion of the client who just entered Treatment Room 3? A scriptwriter who just lost his job? A casting agent down on his luck? A little-known actor about to break out big-time? Or—" Jake paused dramatically, as if facing a television camera—"is it possible that Mr. Steve Farlow from Room 2112 is merely a non-VIP guest from South Dakota enjoying a mountain holiday with his family? An average guy taking advantage of the opportunity to have a relaxing massage in the King's Crown Resort's world-class spa facilities?"

Jake stuck his fist, clenched to hold an imaginary microphone, under Seneca's nose. They were alone behind the spa desk—Kelsey had gotten a call that she was needed in the resort manager's office for a meeting—and they were bored out of their minds.

Seneca pushed Jake's hand away and made a face. "You're the worst."

But she loved it. He was the only person at King's Crown who made her feel normal, even though he constantly made fun of her—at least when Kelsey wasn't around. He flirted with her, told entertaining stories about wacky things that happened at his dad's gas station (and they really were entertaining . . . the guy needed to think about a career in screenwriting, not that writers made any money), and basically kept her from thinking about the fact she'd now watched more than three weeks slip by on the calendar without gaining a single solid lead for her mom.

She still hadn't met Claire's boyfriend. And though she'd had drinks with Gabriela twice, Gaby only wanted to discuss shopping or guys, claiming she didn't want to think about L.A. and "the business" until she had to.

"Patience" had become her mantra this summer, though it was hard to be patient when Mom was estimating what she could get on eBay for her collection of formal gowns.

At least when they spoke last night Mom had agreed to bite the bullet and call her agent today. "I want him to know I'm still here, still very employable," she'd said. "And I'll find a tasteful, subtle way to let him know that he can and will be replaced if he doesn't start doing his job and getting me more auditions. Maybe some commercial work in Japan."

Seneca didn't hold out much hope for anything on that front, though. Axel had too much pull; short of making some miracle connection, Mom wasn't going to find an agent better than her current one. And everyone wanted to do commercial work in Japan. It paid big these days—even Kate Winslet and Brad Pitt had made Japanese ads—so no way would Mom's agent toss that kind of work her way. He'd ask another one of his clients first.

Jake squinted at Seneca, pushing his glasses up with his index finger as he did so. "All right, a different approach is called for today. Apparently Miss Billeray isn't up to her usual Hollywood name-dropping self and cannot participate in today's edition of the 'Tinseltown Tracking Report.' So . . ."

Jake rolled his desk chair a few feet away from Seneca's, spun it around a couple times, then stopped and faced her again. "Hey, Seneca! Great to see you. How's it going this morning? You still have your info desk roommate avoiding you for some unknown reason and your psycho-athlete roommate pissed off because she twisted her ankle yesterday and got reassigned to kitchen duty for the next week while it heals?"

"Go back to the entertainment report, Jake."

"Can't. Clients."

Seneca turned and looked over her shoulder. A tall man in a yellow Lacoste shirt and pressed white shorts stood just outside the spa's glass doors, near the entrance to the beauty salon. He dropped a designer duffel bag to the floor, then crossed his arms and stared down the hall connecting the spa to the rest of the lodge, apparently waiting for someone to join him.

"Elliott Grey," Jake said, as if Seneca hadn't recognized him immediately. "The man with the wimp name but enough money and power to make up for it. Does he have another massage appointment?"

"Not that I noticed." And Seneca would have noticed.

A few minutes later, a buff, fair-haired teenager wearing black gym shorts and a Jimmy Buffett T-shirt strolled up and started talking to Mr. Grey.

"Please don't tell me that's the guy you told me your roommate is going out with," Jake muttered. "Claire's her name, right? The girl who works at the info desk? If that's her Aaron, he has rotten taste in music."

Seneca pulled in her stomach—not that she thought she had one—and straightened her back so she had as close to red carpet posture as she could muster while sitting behind a spa desk. Good thing she'd accidentally and on purpose stained her dumb green King's Crown shirt when she got to the spa this morning and changed into the chic Juicy Couture tracksuit she'd stashed in her locker. Kelsey had grumbled, but there wasn't much she could do. And besides, Seneca was wearing her name tag, so she didn't see the big problem.

"Buffett's cool," she said to Jake. "How can you not like 'Margaritaville'? Or 'Cheeseburger in Paradise'?"

"Because I don't."

The Greys pushed through the glass doors and approached the desk. Seneca blinked as she got a good look at the son.

No way! The blond guy from The Shed—the one who'd bolted after Todd threw up on the bar—was none other than Aaron Grey.

She made sure her smile encompassed both Greys but addressed the father as she processed that little factoid. "Hello, Mr. Grey. How are you today?"

"Wonderful, Seneca. Wonderful." He swiped his membership card through the reader, then smiled at her. "You enjoying your summer here?"

"Who wouldn't? The resort is exquisite." She leaned forward, as if imparting a secret. "I'm so lucky my mom let me come here for the summer. Get away from L.A. for a little while and experience something different, you know?"

"Yes, I'd say you're quite lucky. Though it's awfully humid outside today. I could use a little L.A."

She could feel Jake's desire to make gagging noises at the conversation. Ignoring him, she asked, "Is there anything I can do for you, Mr. Grey? I'm happy to help you with whatever you need."

"Just coming in for a workout with my son, Aaron. Have you met Aaron?"

"Not yet, but we have a number of mutual friends. I've heard very good things." She stood and shook Aaron's hand over the desk. Mr. Grey was impressed, she could tell. Jake, she sensed, not so much. He didn't budge from his chair. "Hi, Aaron. I'm Seneca. Seneca Billeray."

"Jacqueline Billeray's her mom," Jake cut in. "She won an Oscar and everything."

"Oh, Jake," she waved him off, like it was nothing. She'd kick his ass later. Once someone like Elliott Grey knew who you were and who you were related to, you didn't remind him. And she'd made sure he found out about her mom—casually, from Kelsey—the first time he and his wife came in for massages.

"I need to change clothes, so why don't I go on ahead while you sign up for those personal training sessions you mentioned?" Mr. Grey said to Aaron. "Meet me in the weight room when you're done."

Jake stood once Mr. Grey left the reception area. "Seneca, you can handle the personal training signup, right? I need to make sure the towels are stocked in the yoga room before Kelsey gets back from the manager's office."

She made a half-hearted gripe about having him wait so she could help him—didn't want to look like she was angling to be alone with Aaron—but didn't argue when Jake said stocking towels wasn't really a two-person job.

She pulled out the logbook with the schedules for the resort's personal trainers and smiled at Aaron. "Do you know what you want in a trainer?" she asked. "We have several certified trainers on staff with flexible schedules. The best person for you depends largely on your goals."

"I play football, so I'd like someone who can challenge my muscles a little. Help me stay in shape over the summer so I'll be ahead of the curve when practices start up again."

She flipped through the book. "You look like you're in terrific shape already, so I'd recommend Pete." Amanda might be better, but no way was she going to stick Aaron with a female trainer, no matter how good she might be. Pete would do just fine.

Claire could thank her later.

She gave Aaron some proposed times, and he picked out six sessions and filled in the necessary information while Seneca watched. When he finished, she promised to have Pete call him for an introduction as soon as possible.

"It's nice that you're working out with your dad in the meantime," she said. "You two must get along really well."

Aaron shrugged. He had fabulous eyes—a light, clear blue. No wonder Claire was so hung up on him. And no wonder Claire acted so suspicious when Seneca asked about meeting him. If Aaron Grey were *her* boyfriend, she'd be on constant alert for other girls making moves.

"We get along all right. He works a lot."

"Yeah, my mom, too. She's always busy with one project or another." Seneca waited a few, calculated seconds, then added, "She's a big fan of your dad's, you know. Thinks he's worked on some quality projects."

Aaron grinned. "Your mom's no slouch either. I loved her in *After Prague*. It's one of my dad's favorite films, too."

That was the opening Seneca wanted. She mustered her best flirty—but not obviously flirty—voice. "You know, wouldn't it be something if our parents could get together on a project? I bet they'd—"

The spa doors banged open as a UPS guy came in with a sizable box balanced on one shoulder. He dumped it on the desk in front of Seneca, then gave her the electronic signature pad.

Horrid timing.

She signed for the package, then turned her attention back to Aaron as the deliveryman pushed back through the doors.

Aaron was leaning forward, his arms on the counter, but she could tell from his expression that he was about to excuse himself and go exercise. She might not get another chance.

She reached across the desk and put her hand on his wrist. "I know you'll get great results with Pete. You should give me a call and let me know how it goes with football once we're both back in L.A. Maybe we can get our parents together on a project. Wouldn't that be fun?"

Aaron gave her a grin that was absolutely to die for. One that let her know he'd definitely be discussing Jacqueline Billeray with his dad during their workout.

He opened his mouth to say something, but at that exact moment a noise came from the double doors. Aaron took a step back from Seneca, pulling his wrist out from under her hand. "Hey, Claire."

"Hi." She looked from Aaron to Seneca, then back to Aaron. "I didn't know you were going to be here at the resort today."

This was going to be bad. Seneca couldn't mistake the hopefulness on Claire's face at the sight of Aaron. Or the fact that Claire was less than happy about the fact she'd had her hand on Aaron's wrist. But there was something else simmering in the room. A vibe both Aaron and Claire gave off. And in that instant, Seneca *knew*.

They hadn't seen each other in a while. And they hadn't planned to see each other today, even though they were in the same building.

Whoa. No wonder Claire had avoided all her questions about Aaron. They'd broken up, or at least were in the middle of a fight. It must've happened that first night he'd come into town or pretty soon thereafter. That'd explain the pouty look Claire'd had on her face the last few weeks. Why she acted all friendly until the instant Seneca even hinted at the topic of Aaron Grey.

And—now that she thought about it—why Aaron was getting plastered with Todd at The Shed. Otherwise, wouldn't he have still been out on his date with Claire?

And he'd been complaining to Todd about girl trouble, hadn't he?

"Dad asked me to join him for a workout," Aaron told Claire. "I should probably get in there. He's waiting for me."

"Sure. Catch you later."

Claire watched him as he entered the locker room. The moment the door swung shut, she turned on Seneca. "God, Seneca, what is your problem?"

Did Claire just take the Lord's name in vain? "Look, Claire—"

"I know you think he's out of my league. That I'm just some local yokel. I get that. But that doesn't mean that you should hit on him yourself."

"I wasn't hitting on him." Though it'd probably be the smart thing to do, if she wanted to accomplish her goal of hooking her mom up with someone who could rejuvenate her career. But just this morning she'd wondered if she should set her sights on Todd Mirelli. He had connections, he was cute, and he was available. Best of all, it'd drive the Koss sisters mad if she got cozy with him this summer.

Then again, he did hurl all over a very nice bar, and everyone had seen him do it.

"So what were you doing with your hand on Aaron's wrist? Checking his pulse? Were you going to practice your CPR skills next?"

"I was just being friendly, that's all. He was signing up for personal training sessions. I even put him with a male trainer instead of a female one because I figured it'd be doing you a favor."

"Don't do me any favors, Seneca."

"Claire—"

She held up a hand to stop Seneca from saying any more. "I'm leaving."

Claire turned to go, but as she grabbed the door handle Seneca called after her, "Why'd you come down here?"

Seneca could feel the waves of anger coming from Claire, but Claire stopped and turned to look at her anyway. "Marla told me to close up the info desk early. Apparently a big thunderstorm is on its way. They're expecting a lot of lightning and hail starting in an hour or so. Possibly a power outage. Marla wants us to urge guests to stay in their rooms, to keep off the hiking trails and avoid any excursions until it passes. I was supposed to come tell you so you could inform spa clients."

"Oh." Guess that explained why Mr. Grey thought it was so humid outside. The yuck before the storm. "Am I supposed to tell instructors to cancel evening classes?"

"Their discretion."

"I'll let them know." Goddess Yoga was on the schedule for tonight—the first time it wasn't in the middle of her shift—and she'd really hoped to go.

Claire spun around, opened the door, and left. Seneca closed her eyes—how was she possibly going to make this right with Claire?—but started when a noise came from the doorway.

"Oh, Seneca?"

Claire. Maybe she'd realized that she'd jumped to conclusions.

"Yes?"

"You say you weren't hitting on Aaron."

"I wasn't!"

"Whether you were or not, I'm warning you. I see you doing it again and I'll make sure he finds out just how big a bitch you are."

She stormed out, leaving Seneca stunned.

"She didn't mean it."

Seneca sat back down in her black chair, then used her toes to spin it around so she faced Jake, who'd watched who-knows-how-much of the exchange from where he was standing near the men's locker room door.

"She meant it," Seneca said. "And she's right. I *am* a bitch. Not that I was hitting on her boyfriend, because I wasn't. Not really. I don't want to go out with him."

"I know."

"Liar." Seneca shook her head. "You think I was hitting on him, too, but you're being nice."

Jake laughed, then strolled across the room to sit beside Seneca. His leggy gait didn't mesh with the stuffy green polo shirt he was wearing. Neither did the way he slouched in his chair. He was Jimmy Buffett casual, even if he claimed to hate the guy's music.

"I'm sure *most* people would think you were hitting on him. But I know you weren't. You're just a flirt when you want something. You can't help yourself. But that doesn't mean you actually *want* Aaron. You've known him for all of five minutes."

"Gee, thanks. Unable to help myself from flirting. That still makes me sound like a grade-A bitch. And not in the strong, businesslike sense of the word. In the backstabbing, nasty sense that makes every other woman on the planet want to quarantine you."

Jake leaned forward and put his hands on the arms of her chair, spinning her so she looked right into his eyes. For the first time since they'd started working together she could tell that the lean-in wasn't so he could say something snarky about a client or tell a joke.

"The fact you don't want to be thought of as a bitch—the backstabbing kind—tells me that you aren't one. You wouldn't have tried to stop Claire from walking out of here, and you wouldn't be so bothered by it, if you were. You like her. You worry about her. You're a good roommate and a good person, Seneca."

A good person? No one had ever said that to her before.

Well, maybe her mom, but Mom didn't count.

"Jake—"

She didn't finish the question. His expression and the way he was still holding on to her chair told her how serious he was.

She exhaled. How had she not noticed his mouth before? How flat-out sensuous it was? Better than Aaron Grey's or Todd Mirelli's, for certain.

She so wished his dad didn't run an Exxon station. She wished he didn't hate Jimmy Buffett or have hair on his toes.

And she really wished he didn't tease her about her life in L.A. or make fun of her prized Stella McCartney gym bag or the way she thrived on Hollywood gossip, because she wanted to kiss him right now more than she had ever, *ever* wanted to kiss a guy. Just wrap her hand around the back of his head and pull him in and kiss him until neither one of them could breathe and they ached because they wanted each other so badly.

But his dad did run an Exxon station. And he did have hair on his toes. And probably, deep down, he hated everything that was important in her life, even if he didn't hate her.

Seneca straightened in her chair. "Jake, I'm not a good person. I'm shallow. Let's just leave it at that.

Besides, we're about to have company." She smiled in the direction of the door as Kelsey came through with two instructors right behind her. Jake gave Seneca a quick glare that promised he wasn't finished with her, then rolled his chair away from hers.

"So, what's the word, Kelsey?"

"The word, Jake, is that we're going to call anyone who's booked for a spa appointment tonight to see if they'd like to reschedule. I have a feeling we're going to lose electricity—there's a really bad storm blowing in—and that means it'll be impossible to do facials or power any of the equipment. Janice and Cory here"—she glanced at the two instructors who'd entered with her—"are going to call their regulars. Janice is going to cancel the eight p.m. Budokon class, but Cory's going to try to make a go of Goddess Yoga at six thirty."

"Might have to be by candlelight, but it shouldn't be a problem. And I don't mind if it's a small class," the blonde commented. "Were you going to come tonight, Seneca? You'd mentioned that you wanted to try it."

"Definitely." Besides, her roommates might decide to lock her out of the cabin and she'd need to find shelter from the storm somewhere.

May as well be a spa, the official hangout of shallow people.

✳✳✳ Fourteen ✳✳✳

Claire walked back to the cabin with her arms crossed over her stomach, trying not to be ill. How dare Seneca ruin her whole day?

This morning things had been going wonderfully. She'd read from Proverbs when she woke up—passages about trusting in the Lord with all her heart and not trying to make judgment calls based on her own understanding of things. That God would direct her path. Though she wasn't sure about not trusting her own judgment (because didn't God give her that judgment?), the part about God directing her path was reassuring. It helped her realize that things would turn out for the best. And just as Claire had closed her Bible, Drew had come downstairs and made a pot of coffee for them both, even though Claire knew Drew had to be in a foul mood since she couldn't run after hurting her ankle while jogging the day before.

Drew didn't seem to want to talk about her ankle or

how she managed to make it back down the mountain, but she was more chatty than usual, telling Claire that she still wanted to get together to ride mountain bikes in a week or two, when her ankle was better. Drew had even sounded optimistic, saying that she'd only twisted it, that it wasn't a break or even a sprain, so the resort doctor thought she'd heal quickly.

Then today at work she'd had such a great time—handing out brochures about local horseback riding opportunities to a really nice couple from New York, reserving bicycles for a California family who wanted to take the bike path into town, giving maps of the hiking trails to eager guests from Iowa and getting them signed up for an afternoon with Rob—she'd stopped thinking about Aaron for nearly six hours straight.

She'd felt like herself for the first time since Aaron had walked away with a "See ya around, Claire."

She'd felt *good*. Like she might find things to enjoy in life, even if Aaron wasn't part of it. She'd even day-dreamed about the Teen Jam car wash. Not just about how fun it'd be to work in the sunshine and earn money for the Mexico trip, but about the possibility of meeting a new boyfriend there. It hadn't occurred to her until she thought about Delia and Amanda and all their accusations, but it made sense. A guy from Teen

Jam would probably be supportive of the choices she made.

The daydream fizzled the instant she saw Seneca with her hand on Aaron's forearm, giving him the most obvious don't-you-want-me smile she'd ever seen. And worse, Aaron looked like he did, in fact, want her. He was giving Seneca the same smile he'd given her in the restaurant that very first day when he'd followed her to the rest room, hoping to introduce himself.

Every bit of pain she'd felt watching Aaron walk away came back to smack her in the gut, and smack her hard.

"You won't give me what I can't handle, God, I know that," Claire grunted to herself as she took the trail back to cabin number nine. She sent up a mental request for forgiveness for using God's name in vain when she'd yelled at Seneca. That'd been out of line.

But calling Seneca a bitch? She couldn't apologize for that. Not yet. Because in her heart she'd meant it, and God didn't like fake apologies. He *knew* if you were lying to him.

Lying to anyone—let alone to God—would just compound her problem. She'd given Seneca the benefit of the doubt so many times before, had chastised herself for making assumptions about Seneca's intentions. Even defended her to Drew. But this . . . this time, Claire knew what she saw. And she couldn't even begin to ask herself, *What would Jesus do?*

She hugged herself tighter and kept walking, head down.

"Hey, Claire."

Claire's gaze snapped up at the familiar voice. "Todd. What are you doing here?"

He was sitting on the front stoop of her cabin, and it looked like he'd been there a while. His dark brown hair, usually combed just so, looked windblown, and there were marks in the dirt where he'd been making squiggles with the toe of his shoe while he waited.

"This is where you're living for the summer, right?"

"It is." That didn't answer her question. Did someone send him here? Aaron, even? No, if Aaron were interested in making nice he'd come himself. And he wouldn't have been hanging out with Seneca, letting her flirt so blatantly.

"Todd, why are you here? It's nasty and humid out. I doubt you've been sitting here because you were hoping for a house tour. Trust me, the place is not impressive."

That earned her a wry smile. "Look, Claire, I don't want to come off like a stalker or anything but I had to see you. You've been ignoring my calls for a couple months. And you avoided me at your mom and dad's barbeque a couple weeks ago. I can't imagine listening to my dad talk about forest preservation methods at ski resorts was as interesting as you pretended. I'm worried about you."

Claire raised an eyebrow. "*You're* worried about me? Why?"

"Um, yeah! We're *friends*, Claire. At least we used to be. So what gives? You acted strange all spring, but I figured it was 'cause I was dating Ashley Conrad and she was getting so possessive and didn't want me hanging out with any of my female friends. Yet you're still refusing to return my calls now that Ashley and I are splitsville, and I know things went south with you and Aaron 'cause I saw him at The Shed a few weeks ago, on the night you two were supposed to be out to dinner. And I hear he's out nearly every night without you—"

She didn't need to hear about Aaron going places without her. Not now. "Gotcha, Todd. You're worried."

"I'm worried."

"Well, I'm fine."

"Sure. You walk down the path all by your lonesome looking like this"—Todd crossed his arms in front of him and exaggerated a frown—"but you're *fiiiiine*. You're exactly like the Claire Watts I've known all my life. The one who was wickedly funny and popular all through school, until she met Aaron Grey last summer and became not only wickedly funny and popular, but ended up spending junior year as one of the hardest partiers in school. Dancing on a table drunk when Aaron was here for spring break, if I do recall. And I do. Vividly. I think I even saw your panties when you flashed—"

"Thanks for that wonderful memory, Todd, but—"

He held up a finger to stop her. "But you don't do that anymore. You haven't been seen out in months. So I'm thinking that things with you have changed and you might want to chat with an old friend. Someone who's known you forever and you can trust. And who's worried."

"Someone who needs a pal to party with and isn't happy with the pickings this summer?"

He used his palms to push himself up so he was facing her. "Well, Dahlia and Violet Koss are in town. You remember them? I think I could find a party if I wanted one. I could just follow them."

Claire rolled her eyes. She remembered them from spring break, when she'd met them at a party. Their dad had a gigantic house at the edge of town, maybe even bigger than Todd's parents' place. The Koss sisters were just like Seneca, only meaner. "So which one are you interested in? Dahlia or Violet?"

"Please. It's a wonder they have enough brain power between them to function."

She laughed. And it felt good. It felt *normal*. "I take it you knocked before you plopped yourself down on my doorstep?"

"If anyone's in there, they didn't answer."

"Well, Seneca isn't there, because I just saw her. And Drew's probably still at work. I got to leave my shift a little early with the storm coming." She pulled out her key, opened the door, and waved him in.

Probably not the smartest move—she still didn't trust him a hundred percent—but he was right. He'd been her friend a long time, and it wasn't like he could force her to go to The Shed or any of their other fave places. She'd just decline politely and send him on his way.

"Oh, about Drew," he began. "Some guy named Rob came to the door. He was asking if Drew was here. Said she hurt her ankle and he wanted to make sure she was all right. Seemed like he was concerned. I told him I didn't think anyone was here."

"I'll make sure Drew gets the message." She flicked on the light and spread her arms in an all-encompassing gesture. "Told you. It's not exactly ready for *Architectural Digest* to come through."

He glanced around, taking in the television, coffee-maker, and couches, then looking up the staircase. His back to her, he asked, "When you said Seneca, did you mean Seneca Billeray?"

"That's my roommate." Unfortunately.

"Ah."

Claire dropped onto the couch. "'Ah'? What does that mean? You know her?"

"Know *of* her. You'll like this. You know how Dahlia and Violet have this thing about their dad being in the music industry while most people who summer here are in film and television?"

When Claire nodded, Todd continued, "Well, I guess the Koss girls ran into Seneca downtown right after she got here. They know her because her mom used to live with Axel Randolph—"

"That producer guy with the house?"

"Yeah, *that* house. "

Huh. She hadn't realized that. Probably escaped her drunken notice last year.

"Anyway, when Dahlia and Violet saw Seneca they invited her to their dad's birthday party at The Final Run. They wanted to kiss her ass, basically. But at the party, Frankie Milhone took an interest in Seneca."

Great. Apparently *every* guy in town took an interest in Seneca. "And?"

"Dahlia's had it bad for Frankie for years. So Dahlia

and Violet dragged her away from Frankie and threw it in Seneca's face that she's an employee here, not a guest. They're spreading rumors around town that Seneca's mom's career is in the toilet. Total social power play for them, you know?"

Claire felt a niggle of guilt for calling Seneca a bitch. But just a niggle. "How do you know all this?"

"About them spreading rumors, or about what happened the night with Frankie?"

"The night with Frankie." Seneca never let on that anything like that had happened to her. She was out at bars every night meeting up with friends she said she'd met during other summers here. Some were people Claire knew, some weren't. But Seneca never once mentioned getting dissed by anyone the way the Koss sisters had apparently done.

"I was there. Well, sort of. I was here at King's Crown when Dahlia and Violet dropped off Seneca. They offered me a ride to The Shed, so I took it. But when I got in the car there was a cell phone in the backseat. I handed it up to Dahlia thinking it was hers and she threw it out. Right onto the parking lot asphalt. When I asked her why, she just laughed and said it belonged to Seneca Billeray, and it served Seneca right for letting Frankie flirt with her when everyone knew she liked Frankie."

"Wow." Seneca seemed to have a lot of practice flirting with guys other girls liked.

"That's what I thought. And Seneca's apparently worked really hard to avoid them when she's out bar hopping. Anyway"—he sat next to Claire on the sofa and gave her a playful elbow in the ribs—"I'm not here to gossip about your roommate. I came to talk to you. Preferably before either of your roommates come back. Or the storm gets here. My mom will kill me if I'm on the road when it's hailing. There's supposed to be hail."

"I heard."

"So what gives with you and Aaron?"

Claire could tell from his voice that he was sincerely worried and that she could trust him. But she wasn't ready to spill. Not while she was still figuring things out for herself.

"We're going through a rough patch. That's all."

"And that's why you're not talking to *me*?" He said it in a laughy-laughy way, but Claire could tell that, underneath his teasing, his feelings had been hurt. Even if he hung out with the hard-core party crowd, they'd known each other all their lives. They'd always had a bond that transcended the summer types.

"I'm sorry. It's just—I'm trying to figure out what I want from the relationship. And I need to figure out who

I am and what I want in life in general first. It's . . . well, it's been kinda hard."

"I'm sorry. I wish you'd told me earlier. I'd have been there for you."

"Like Ashley would have let me get close."

"Touché. Which reminds me. Part of the reason I've wanted to see you is to tell you what really happened with Ashley—"

"Totally your business," Claire said, waving her hands to stop him from saying more than he should.

"No, 'cause the more I think about it, the more I think it might be important to you and Aaron."

"How?"

"Everyone thinks I broke up with Ashley because she's so possessive. That's even what I told her. But it was only part of the reason." He sucked in his lower lip for a moment, then said, "The thing is, I've decided I can't live that way anymore. Hanging out with the serious party crowd from L.A., I mean. Not the way you have to if you're going out with one of them. I still go out—I mean, knowing that crowd is really helpful for promoting the ski resort—but I can't handle spending every weekend so blitzed I can't function. It's easier for me to scoot out of the bars and clubs and stuff and go home early if I don't have to drag Ashley with me."

Cautiously, Claire asked, "And this is what you think happened with me and Aaron?"

"Haven't seen you out anywhere. So I was wondering if spring break was . . . I dunno . . . if it kind of woke you up the way it woke *me* up. I spent the week after spring break trying to get over the worst hangover in the history of the world and decided it wasn't worth it. Of course, I got over it and went drinking again when the summer crowd showed up, thinking I could keep myself in check."

"But?"

A flush crept into Todd's cheeks. "I got out of control. Put it this way: Mikey's exiled me from The Shed for the rest of the summer."

Claire stared at him. "What'd you do?!"

"You don't want to know. Let's just say I was sufficiently embarrassed to give the shit up for good."

A clap of thunder shook the cabin, jarring them from the conversation. "Wow, that was loud," Claire commented, even though it was probably the biggest "duh" statement she'd made in ages.

After a moment she met Todd's gaze. "Look, thanks for telling me about you and Ashley. I'm not really up for spilling my guts about Aaron, but hearing you say all that . . . well, it makes me feel better."

"Keep it under wraps, okay? I still need to make nice with all those L.A. people, even if I don't party with them like I used to."

"No problem." Wasn't like she wanted to see any of them and gossip, anyway.

Todd put an arm around her shoulders and gave her a quickie hug, then let go. "I hope everything with Aaron works out whichever way is better for *you*."

"Thanks."

The wind picked up outside, causing the screen on the window nearest the stairs to rattle.

"I'd better get going," Todd said. "But call me, Claire. Seriously. If you want to go out anywhere, I'll take you. We can hang with the crowd from school or not. Go the party route—without the alcohol, if that's okay—or just go low-key. I get the feeling you'd rather go low-key, but no pressure. I think it'd be good for you to socialize a little."

"We'll see." His eyes were still filled with concern, so she added, "But I'll definitely call. And don't worry about me in the meantime, okay?"

He stood and walked to the door. She held it open, looking at the sky. It'd gotten a lot darker just in the few minutes Todd had been inside the cabin with her.

He stepped down into the dirt in front of the stoop,

then put his hands in his pockets and turned to face her. "Can I give you some advice, Claire?"

"Like I can stop you."

"I know you loved Aaron. You probably still love Aaron. But you've got to take care of yourself first. Do what you think is right for you. No matter what happens with him, you won't be alone. You've got a lot of friends."

"That's a nice thing to say, but I think we both know that's not true." Her old crowd from school didn't trust her anymore, not since she'd ignored them all year to hang out with Aaron. And the Teen Jam girls obviously didn't trust her either. Amanda and Delia stared at her every time she saw them in the cafeteria or walking around the lodge like she was Satan incarnate, out to play some dirty trick on them.

He reached up and mussed her hair. "Okay, maybe you don't have friends, plural. But you've got me."

She grinned and shook her head. "Thanks, Todd."

Past him, about forty feet away, Drew was hobbling along the path, heading for the cabin.

He followed Claire's gaze. "Is that Drew?"

"Yep."

Drew smiled at them both as she approached. After introducing herself to Todd she ducked into the cabin.

"She respects your personal space. Seems like a good

roommate," Todd said as he pulled his car keys from the front pocket of his shorts.

"Yeah, she is."

He smiled. "Good. You deserve it."

A raindrop hit Claire's head, right at her part. Todd waved, reminded her one more time to call if she needed anything, then turned and jogged up the path toward the lodge.

Claire watched him enter the lodge by the back door—presumably to cut through to the main parking lot—at the same time she saw Seneca exit. No mistaking that it was Seneca, even from this distance. Her cutesy baby blue tracksuit gave her away.

Well, that and the quick backward glance she gave Todd. Did Seneca have to check out *every* guy on the planet?

Claire went into the cabin and shut the door.

God must be filling her with forgiveness because she resisted the urge to flip the lock and block the door with something heavy.

❖ FIFTEEN *❖*

"That Todd guy seemed cool," Drew said after Claire closed the cabin door behind her. "Hope I didn't interrupt anything."

She'd been walking to the cabin—carefully, since going downhill seemed to bother the ankle more than anything else—and noticed Claire talking to someone on the front porch too late to change direction and give them privacy. Not that there was anywhere else she could go with the rain coming; other staff members were either hustling to secure the outdoor furniture and reassure guests or to get home. It'd been a relief to discover the guy at the door wasn't Claire's precious Aaron. Maybe this meant Claire had friends around town who cared about her enough to swing by and try and lift her spirits. And maybe, unlike Drew's mom, Claire would listen to those around her.

But another relationship . . . yech. Drew hoped not.

Claire needed to learn to stand on her own for a while. "Needy" would be a bad trait for Claire to develop.

It was bad enough she'd acted that way herself with Rob. But Claire . . . well, Claire didn't seem to recognize how dangerous needy could be.

"You didn't interrupt anything. Todd's a friend from high school. One of my neighbors, actually. He just stopped in to say hi." Claire walked over to the couch, where Drew was sitting with her ankle propped up on the edge. Drew made a move to lower it but Claire waved her off, indicating she was happy standing. There was a tinge of anger in her voice as she said, "Seneca's on her way down the path, so if you hadn't interrupted us, she would have."

"Uh-oh. What's going on there?"

Lines of annoyance crisscrossed Claire's forehead. "Long story. I'll get over it."

"It'll have to be quick. We're all going to be trapped in the cabin together tonight. No way she'll be out barhopping with her fake ID in this weather. It'll muss her hair and get water drops on her precious Dolly-and-whoever skirt."

"Dolce & Gabbana," Claire replied, the laughter in her voice reassuring Drew. "Not that it matters. Bet she spends the night holed up in the bathroom giving herself a pedicure or another of those green facials."

Drew stretched to the floor to pick up a copy of *Shape* magazine that'd been left there earlier. "We can only hope."

"Oh, Todd said that while he was waiting for me Rob stopped by. He seemed worried about your ankle. You might want to give him a call."

Drew tried to look nonchalant as she flipped magazine pages. "Okay. I'll talk to him." When she had to. She had no idea what to say to him anymore.

The front door opened and Seneca rushed inside, her hair fluffed out from the wind. "It's really windy and it's about to pour," she said as she shut the door behind her. "Sucks."

Master of the obvious, that girl. "Got plans tonight, Seneca?" Drew asked.

"Actually, yes." Seneca sounded psyched. "I was hoping that we could all do something together."

Taking care to pick the right words, Drew said, "I don't think we'll be able to go anywhere."

"I'm busy," Claire grumbled.

Seneca shot Claire a look Drew couldn't read. Something had definitely gone down between those two. Hoping to diffuse the situation, Drew asked Seneca what she had in mind. Not that she was all fired up to do anything with Seneca, but talking distracted her from the pain in her ankle. And from thinking about what'd happened with Rob up on the trail. How understanding he'd been when she'd blurted out everything about her dad, how he'd helped without babying her on the walk back down to the lodge. How he'd smiled and told her everything would be all right when he left her with the lodge's doctor. How she'd felt like such a crybaby idiot when she finally got back to her cabin.

But most of all, how great it'd felt to relax into him, to have her head tucked against his shoulder, to have his arm around her and feel the rise and fall of his chest against her cheek.

Yeah, even Seneca's self-absorbent yakking would be a welcome distraction. Letting her thoughts dwell on that afternoon with Rob meant nothing but trouble.

The one good thing about having been assigned to help in the employee kitchen until her ankle healed was that she'd been able to avoid him. No way did she want to see him with the oh-that's-so-awful-you-poor-thing look she'd gotten from everyone back at school since her dad was killed. Not that he'd given any indication he would do that to her, but she didn't want to risk it.

"Well, you guys probably heard that this is supposed to be a really nasty thunderstorm. Hail, high winds, the whole thing—"

"So what's your bright idea?" Drew didn't need the full weather report. Not with Claire standing at the end of the couch looking like she'd rival the storm in ferocity if Seneca dared utter one word too many.

"The instructors at the spa were told that it was up to their discretion whether or not they wanted to hold class tonight. Cory's scheduled to do a class called Goddess Yoga that sounds great. It's the kind of class where we can get a good workout but relax and let go of stress, too. Cory says she'll do the class even if it ends up being by candlelight, and—"

"Ankle. Can't do it." Which sucked.

"And I'm busy," Claire repeated.

Seneca grinned at Drew. "I mentioned your ankle to Cory. She says she can modify the moves so you don't put any pressure on it. It'll give you a good upper body work-out, especially the sun salutations. Might cheer you up to get some exercise."

Drew had to admit that it sounded like exactly what she needed. Even though it'd only been a couple days, kitchen duty was making her feel as claustrophobic as she had on that heinous bus ride from Kansas. No way was she going to go without Claire, though. What if none of the resort guests showed for the class and it ended up being just her and Seneca?

Drew eyed Claire. "You sure you can't change your plans? I'll go if you go. It'll beat sitting here in the dark with flashlights and nothing to do but stare at each other. If we went to yoga we could just zone out and listen to what's-her-name—"

"Cory."

"—talk about warrior poses and body alignment. It'll make the evening pass a lot faster," Drew finished.

Claire didn't look convinced. "It's called Goddess Yoga? They don't talk about worshipping goddesses, I hope, because I couldn't—"

"No," Seneca replied. "No pagan rituals or devil worship, so I'm sure you'd be fine, Claire. Please? It'll be good for us."

Claire looked less than enthusiastic but finally admitted that taking a yoga class would be better than sitting in the cabin all night.

"We've only got twenty minutes before class starts," Seneca said, tapping the spot on her wrist where a watch would normally be, "so we ought to get changed." She took a couple steps to her left and peeked out the front window. "It's still just a drizzle out there, but the sky's really dark. Maybe we should grab our clothes and change in the spa locker room so we're not stuck outside when it really starts coming down."

"What about dinner?" Claire asked.

"We can eat afterward," Seneca answered. "Don't want to do yoga on a full stomach, anyway."

Drew pushed herself off the couch. "Okay, let's get going."

Drew wasn't sure if Claire would move from where she stood. However, after rolling her eyes, Claire followed Drew upstairs and jammed a water bottle and some loose-fitting workout clothes into a backpack while Drew did the same.

Fifteen minutes later, they were sitting on mats in the resort's yoga studio, listening to the rain thump against the skylights overhead. Cory introduced herself to Drew and Claire, then loaded batteries into a portable CD player while they waited for the rest of the class to arrive.

Drew's entire yoga experience constituted of some stretches her cross-country coach had them all do after their daily runs. Poses he claimed would help keep them flexible, improve their balance, and prevent injury. But she'd never taken any formal classes. Too expensive, and too hard to get Mom motivated to drive her to yet another athletic endeavor. Plus, the classes offered in Leavenworth sounded way too woo-woo and touchy-feely-sensitive for her to consider.

But she had to admit, now that she was here—at a class

bound to be woo-woo—the studio setting appealed to her. The hardwood floors, the soft music, the low lights.

Almost made her forget about her breakdown in front of Rob. And almost—but not quite—made her forget she'd positioned her mat in between Seneca and Claire in an effort to ease the tension between them. Claire had taken the peacemaker role often enough between Drew and Seneca the last few weeks; Drew figured she owed Claire one.

"Well, it looks like a class of three tonight," Cory said. "Hope you don't mind."

"As long as you don't," Seneca replied, cringing as a rumble of thunder shook the room. "Aren't you worried about that typhoon out there?"

"I doubt there's ever been a typhoon in Colorado," Cory said as she set her water bottle on the floor near the front of the room. "And I love storms. Perfect time to do yoga. Plus, my boyfriend's working for two more hours and he's my ride. I'd be sitting in the main lobby bored out of my skull if I cancelled class."

She rolled her mat out at the front of the room, warning Drew to take it easy and let her know if her ankle bothered her so she could give her some modifications for the poses. She sat cross-legged at the front of the room, her back straight, and started out by showing them how to breathe during class. Long, deep breaths in, pulling air as far into their lungs as possible, then exhaling slowly and completely, concentrating on the sound it made.

It didn't feel like exercise to Drew, but it did feel good.

Cory had them stand, stretch their hands over their heads into what she called mountain pose, then bend at the waist and drop forward so their hands were near the floor. As they repeated the move Cory spoke softly. "While we do yoga we focus inward, on our bodies, on how we feel. We stay rooted in the present. We let go of all that has bothered us in the past and set aside anything that worries us about the future. We stay in the moment."

Easier said than done, Drew thought as she reached for the ceiling once more, letting her ribcage expand with each inhalation. But she was already a lot less stressed than if she'd spent the evening sitting on the sofa in the cabin.

Cory led them through a series of sun salutations, walking between the girls after the first one to make sure they were positioned correctly and that Drew wasn't putting too much weight on her ankle. As Cory returned to the front of the room a boom of thunder caused the lights to flicker.

"Uh-oh," Seneca whispered.

"Hold that pose," Cory said in the same calm tone she'd used to talk them through the breathing lessons. "I have candles in holders ready to go. It'll make for a peaceful class."

She talked them through the next few poses as she lit the candles, then led them through another series of sun salutations, this time followed by prayer twists to each side. Drew had to admit that, even though her own poses were modified, Seneca had the right idea by asking them to attend class. As Drew turned to each side she could see that Claire and Seneca also looked much more relaxed than when they'd arrived.

Cory continued. "It's appropriate that there are three of you here tonight because the theme of this class—Goddess Yoga—comes from the concept of the Three Goddesses, also known as the Three Fates, who show up in the mythology of various cultures. The Norse, the Greeks, the Romans, even the Hindus, all held to the philosophy that there were three goddesses who determined the course of life for each person on Earth. The three represented the past, the present, and the future. As we go into our series of triangle poses and you stretch your bodies and quiet your minds I'd like you to reflect on those three aspects of life, and think about how—on your own personal journey through this world—each of those aspects of life affects the others."

Personal journey? To Drew the phrase signaled that the woo-woo hour was about to begin in earnest.

The music gradually morphed from an Enya-like melody to a slow, rhythmic drumbeat, and Cory talked them through getting into triangle pose, asking each of them to put their right foot behind them at a ninety-degree angle and their left foot forward. Once they felt balanced, she had them turn to the side and reach up to the ceiling with one hand while resting the other on the floor, near their ankle. Drew modified the pose slightly and found that it was more comfortable than she'd imagined. She focused on her breathing the way Cory had instructed them to do and felt her quad muscles doing their thing, holding her up, giving her a sense of peace.

If she couldn't run, this was definitely the next best thing. Her legs were going to feel this tomorrow.

"As you relax into this pose, be aware of the strength of your thighs and your core—your core being the area in your middle that supports the rest of your body. By doing the triangle pose you're building a strong foundation, one that will carry you through each day feeling physically strong. Now, as you feel your body getting stronger, let your mind wander back to an occurrence in your past—

an event that upset you or an action you regret. Ask yourself, Is this occurrence that bothered you from the past something that you can control in the present?"

Drew closed her eyes, instantly picturing her dad's light brown hair and the way his face looked when he hadn't shaved yet. The day the Death Squad came to the door and she knew she'd never get to talk to him again. That he wouldn't be at her graduation, wouldn't help her pick a college. Wouldn't go on walks around the perimeter of the post's golf course with her after dinner ever again.

Everything that had upset her since that day—people giving her looks in the halls at school, school administrators endlessly asking about her family life, her mother's whacked behavior—all resulted from Dad's death.

And that wasn't something she could control.

After thirty or forty seconds Cory had them reverse their feet and repeat the pose on the other side. She encouraged them to feel the stretch through their hips and spines, then said, "In all the legends about the Three Fates it was acknowledged that the past is out of the hands of humans. It is what it is. What's important is for us to acknowledge the past and to understand that, even if it was difficult, that past shaped us into who we are at present." Cory's voice was soft, melding with the rhythm of the drums and the rat-a-tat of thick raindrops striking the roof above them. "Once your mind is clear of the burdens of the past, you can focus on becoming strong in the present. Learning to make the most of the present, in turn, will make you strong in the future. The three—past, present, and future—are inextricably tied together, just as the Three Goddesses were inextricably tied together."

Drew almost bit her tongue. What a load of bull. Yeah, past and present and future were tied together, but goddesses didn't have anything to do with it.

It was called time. And the passage thereof.

Cory had them take two more deep breaths, then coached them into what she described as a revolved triangle pose. "Oftentimes, the bad things that happened to us in the past make us angry. They might also make us sad or frustrated. Those negative feelings drive what we do in the present. But when you come to yoga you are choosing to bring peace into your present. To strengthen your body and mind and to let go of those negative things in your past that cause you to stumble if you continue to hold onto them."

The damned bear caused me to stumble.

Though she might have seen the bear earlier if she hadn't been so distracted thinking about Mom and their depressing phone conversation. And she wouldn't have fallen apart quite so badly in front of Rob—or spent the last couple days regretting her outburst—if she hadn't been so upset.

They went through a series of warrior poses, then practiced eagle pose, where they wrapped one leg around the other and focused on balance. It was a pose Drew couldn't do on her injured ankle, but Cory proposed a two-footed modification that felt pretty good.

As they came out of the pose, stretched, then did the pose again, Cory said, "Different cultures told varied stories about the Three Fates, or the Three Goddesses. But most of them felt that the key lesson behind the stories is that it is important to act mindfully as we go through each day and to act in a way that is pleasing to the gods."

Claire made a coughing noise beside her, which nearly made Drew crack up. Cory had them straighten, then do another sun salutation as she added, "That probably doesn't sound like it applies to our lives in the way it did to those in ancient times. Most people living in the twenty-first century don't worship ancient gods or worry about pleasing them."

"We sure don't," Claire mumbled, and Drew mentally echoed the sentiment.

"However," Cory continued in the same calm voice as before, "the basic concept—that we can only control how we feel and act in the present, and that living mindfully in the present will prepare us for a better future—is a good one. So, when you come to yoga and you use your mind to control your breath and sink into each pose, your mind naturally clears. Your body becomes stronger, you become more aware of how you feel about the events of your day, and of how you treat others and react to them. You learn to let go of all the negative energy from the past. You realize how wonderful that feels."

A thunderclap sounded outside and the lights flickered again, then went out, leaving them in the candlelight.

Cory's voice had a smile in it as she told them to stand and come back to mountain pose. "We start and end each session here, in mountain pose. This is your center. As you leave this studio and go through your day remember how you feel—both in your body and in your mind—at this moment. How relaxed and clear you feel. How unburdened. When you are bothered by something in the course of your day, mentally bring yourself back to mountain pose. It will help you order your chaotic thoughts and live in the present. To be as strong as a mountain."

She did one final stretch with them, then placed her hands together near her heart, closed her eyes, bowed her head, and wished them *"namaste."* *"Namaste,"* she explained, "is a greeting we give to each other at the end of each yoga class. It means all that is good in my soul recognizes and honors to all that is good in your soul. It is an acknowledgment of our timelessness and that all people are of one heart."

More woo-woo. But Drew liked the sound of the word and repeated it in her head. *Naa-maaa-stay. Namaste.* It'd be a good one to say to herself when she was running. A head-clearing, focused word.

"Thanks, Cory, this was great," Seneca said as Cory went to turn off the CD player. "I can see why guests who are here on vacation love this class. It's a perfect time for them to reinvigorate themselves."

"Exactly," Cory said, grinning. "I structure the class to be a good introduction to basic yoga poses, so if someone wants a more athletic style of yoga, they can progress to that after taking this class. Or if they'd rather do something more contemplative and slow, they can move from this class to one done in a gentler style."

"I wasn't expecting to enjoy this so much," Claire admitted. "Thank you. I'm definitely coming back."

"Me too," Seneca added.

Drew didn't say anything, but she knew she'd also be back. At least until her ankle healed and she could get back out to the trails. Her shoulders, arms, and legs felt like they'd had a good workout, but at the same time, she was relaxed and loose all over.

Another boom of thunder sounded nearby. "You three shouldn't walk back to your cabins yet," Cory said. "Not with the thunder and lightning. The employee cafeteria is still open. Did you get dinner?"

"Not yet," Claire answered.

"Eat a light meal," Cory warned. "Nothing too heavy tonight. And get plenty of water." She rolled up her mat and all three girls did the same, taking them to a corner where a number of rolled mats stood on end, ready for the next class. "I'm sure only the emergency lighting will be on in the cafeteria and the locker room. You girls all right if I head out to the main lobby to meet my boyfriend?"

They told her it was no problem. Drew opened the locker room door, and sure enough, low-level emergency lighting illuminated the area. Cory blew out the candles in the yoga studio, then walked ahead of them through the locker room.

"You guys want to change before dinner?" Seneca asked as they grabbed their things.

Drew adjusted her ponytail holder, which had come loose during class. "I'm good."

"Me too," Claire answered. "I'm not trying to impress anyone."

"Okay. Um, you guys go ahead if you want. I'm going to go to the rest room first."

Seneca ducked through the doorway leading to the toilet stalls as Cory waved good-bye, then headed toward the main lodge. Drew glanced at Claire. Claire, who'd looked so happy during class, stole a look in the direction of the toilets and sighed. "We should probably wait for Seneca. Kind of spooky in here with the power out."

"You don't have to wait," Seneca called from the stalls. "I work here. I'd be fine even if it were pitch-black."

"We're waiting," Drew called back. These two needed to get over whatever it was between them or they'd be awful to live with for the rest of the summer.

"Come on, guys," Drew said once Seneca washed her hands and rejoined them. "Let's eat, drink, and be merry."

✳✳ SIXTEEN ✳✳

Seneca could feel Claire's discomfort as they walked in silence past the line of polished maple lockers and benches, all empty and waiting for the next day's guests.

Couldn't either one of them take the hint when she'd ducked into the rest room? Why couldn't they have gone on without her? She'd have caught up eventually.

She'd felt so good during yoga. All Cory's talk about letting the past go made her determined to apologize to Claire, to promise not to do anything that could possibly be construed as flirting with any guy Claire might be interested in. Cory was right. You needed to make the most of your present, and Claire was a big part of her present. They were going to be living together for two more months and they needed to get along.

Maybe even be friends.

Seneca took a deep breath. She wanted to be Claire's friend. And not just because Claire knew the right people and wore the right clothes. Claire was just . . . Claire.

But wording her apology in a way Claire would find convincing might take some doing. If the feelings simmering between Claire and Aaron were as raw as Seneca guessed, Claire wasn't going to be willing to listen to a generic "I'm sorry." She'd have been too hurt by what she witnessed when she came to the spa earlier.

She needed a few minutes alone to think. And she couldn't even get it in a bathroom stall.

Drew pushed open the locker room door. The spa lobby was darker than the locker room, its only light coming from the emergency lights in the hallway leading to the main lodge. Claire reached the glass door first, holding it open for Drew and Seneca to pass through.

Was that a noise coming from the men's locker room? Seneca turned, straining her eyes to see across the dark spa lobby.

Had to be her imagination. Just the storm blowing outside.

"Seneca, you coming?" Drew asked from the doorway.

She started to turn and follow but the door to the men's locker room opened. A figure emerged, backlit by the locker room's emergency lights.

"Seneca?" The voice was familiar. "You just finishing yoga class?"

"Jake?"

"Yeah. Sorry if I scared you guys. Weird in here without the power, isn't it?"

"What are you doing?" Seneca asked. Hadn't he gone home hours ago?

"Can't find my wallet. Thought I might've left it in the locker room."

Seneca turned to Claire and Drew. "I'll catch up with you guys in a sec, all right?"

Claire shrugged and started walking.

Drew waited a breath, then whispered to Seneca, "She'll get over it. We'll see you in a minute," before following Claire down the hall toward the main lodge.

Jake sauntered closer, hands jammed into the pockets of his cargo shorts. "I take it Claire's still ticked off?"

"And she's not subtle about it, either." Seneca walked to the door of the women's locker room and propped it open so more light entered the lobby. "If you left your wallet here it's going to be hard to find without a little more light."

"Tell me about it." Jake mimicked her action, propping open the door to the men's locker room. "I should have brought a flashlight. Didn't think about it. Power was on at the gas station when I left."

"You think your wallet could be on the desk?"

"I'm not sure. I took it out right before my spa shift ended to break a ten for Mr. Grey. He wanted to buy some trail mix out of the machine when he finished his workout. I was in the locker room wiping down the sinks when he asked. I swear I put it right back in my pocket, though."

"In other words, you have no idea where it is?"

Jake brushed against her as he walked behind the desk. He smelled like rain and gasoline, and his damp hair clung to his forehead. "I'm not sure. I could have set it down in the locker room. Or maybe on the desk. Could've fallen out of my pocket. All I know is that I didn't have it when I got to the station to work, and it's not in my car."

Seneca frowned. "You worked at the gas station after you left here?"

Jake ran his hand along the surface of the desk, around the computer terminal. "Only for two hours. Dad had a guy whose kid has the flu, so I told him I could cover if the guy wanted to go home early."

"But . . . in the rain?"

"People need gas in the rain, Seneca."

Seneca shook her head, then walked behind the desk. Jake wore a dark T-shirt emblazoned in white with the words CAMARILLO STREET EXXON. The letters were so bright, she could read them even in this light. She grabbed a handful of shirt near the hem and squeezed, which sent water splashing to the floor. "This is awful. You're soaked."

He grabbed her hand and pulled his shirt free. "I'll dry."

"Jake—"

"Well, lookee here. You're holding my hand, Seneca."

"Oh, stop it. You grabbed it." This was definitely flirting. Major flirting. Not at all the same as when they were working together in the daylight, knowing Kelsey was within hearing range.

"You were wringing out my shirt."

"You're soaked."

His face was only a few inches from hers. "You're concerned about me, aren't you?"

"Of course. You're going to make yourself sick. And you don't have your wallet."

"Just like you were concerned about Claire earlier."

"If you get sick, I'm going to be stuck working here alone is all."

Did that joke sound as forced to him as it felt to her?

"And," he continued, ignoring her lame attempt at humor, "when I told you that you're a good person this afternoon, I think you wanted to kiss me. In fact, I'm positive."

She needed to keep him from saying more, sensed that something big was about to happen. But deep inside, part of her wanted to hear his words. Wanted to see what he'd do when they were alone and in the dark, bordered by the desk on one side and the wall on the other.

A low rumble of thunder echoed outside, followed by a quick flash of lightning. She stared at Jake, unable to move. "You're still holding my hand."

"You didn't answer my question."

"You didn't ask a question. You made a statement. I'm choosing to ignore it."

He moved closer; she could feel the heat from his body. "Ignore it at your own peril."

"At my own peril? You're the one who won't be able to find your wallet with your hand occupied like that. There's no peril for me."

She couldn't see Jake's eyes to get a read on him. His glasses were misted, causing the light coming from the open locker room doors to reflect her own image back at her.

But then he grinned. That she could see.

"I have plenty of time to find my wallet. It's not going anywhere. But if I'm holding your hand, then you can't go anywhere, either."

"Jake—"

"You wanted to kiss me before, didn't you? And to be clear—yes, that is a question."

She forced herself to relax, to keep him from seeing how unsettled he made her. "Yes. I did want to kiss you. But I exercised my better judgment and I didn't."

Jake eased his fingers from hers and put his hand on his hip, then put his other hand on the desktop, casual as could be.

Good.

But then, without warning, he leaned in and kissed her. *Really* kissed her.

Seneca closed her eyes and kissed him back.

He wasn't even hugging her or touching her—just leaning on the desk and kissing her. And he still smelled like gasoline.

But damnit, she wanted him to keep right on doing it. Because whoa, mamma-mamma-mamma, did the guy know what he was doing.

He nudged her mouth open with his. Subtle, sexy, delicious. Seneca wanted to melt into the floor and take him with her.

A drip of water from his hair hit her forehead. He raised his head enough to kiss it away, then leaned back, giving her the smug look of a gambler who'd bet on a long shot and won.

"Still think you exercised your better judgment?"

She crossed her arms in front of her. What point was he trying to prove here? "So kissing you is great. Phenomenal, even. You might've made me *swoon*. So what?"

He laughed aloud. "So what?"

"Yeah, so what? Jake, I'm shallow. I told you. We come from very different places. It doesn't matter how much I like you or how much fun we have here at work. And it doesn't matter if you're the best kisser in the entire universe—"

"Oh, yeah?"

"That's not what I meant! The bottom line is that I'm going to end up hurting you. So, yes, I used my better judgment not kissing you this afternoon. And I don't think we should do it again. I'll just end up hurting you."

"You don't give me enough credit. I'm tougher than you think. Frankly, you don't give yourself enough credit either, Seneca. You're not half as shallow as you claim to be."

"Quick, tell me who Tory Burch is."

He took off his glasses and used his shirt to wipe them off. Didn't look like it was helping, though. The shirt was too wet. "A piano player. She has red hair and sings."

"Wrong. That's Tori Amos. Tory Burch is a fashion designer."

"Okay. So—"

"How about Christophe? Roberto Cavalli? Bobbi Brown? Ever heard of them?"

He slid his glasses back on. "Nope."

"A famous hair stylist, a fashion designer, and a cosmetics company founder. And—"

"Whoopee." He twirled a finger in the air. "So you could sweep the style category of *Jeopardy!*, if they even have such a thing. And this makes you shallow how?"

"Because those things matter to me. I need to know them, so I read every style magazine I can. Just like I need to know who's who in L.A., so I read *Variety* as often as humanly possible. It's stuff that's completely meaningless to the rest of the world, but it's my life."

Seneca clenched her teeth so hard it hurt. Couldn't he see how terribly this would turn out? If she kissed him again, she wouldn't want to stop. But they'd have to stop, and it'd kill him.

It'd kill *her*.

No one ever gave her such a rock-your-world kiss in her entire life. But some relationships just weren't in the natural order of things.

"That stuff only matters on the surface, Seneca. I

know what you do all day. You hustle the Hollywood types who come in here, but it's not because you're impressed with them. It's because you're trying to help out your mother. I might be some guy who works at the gas station and can't tell what brand of shoes you're wearing, but you think I don't see what you're doing while you're working the desk here? Or that I don't hear people talking when they come into the station to pay for their fill-up or buy gum and a cup of coffee? I know what happened with your mom and that movie guy last summer because everyone in town was talking about it. And I know he has a lot of pull and that has to have hurt your mom's career. If wearing the right clothes or knowing the right people helps your mom, then I don't think it's shallow to want that kind of surface dressing. There are people who go to Yale or Harvard just for the school's name, and no one tells them they're being shallow. I don't see the difference."

Seneca took a step back from Jake. "It's just . . . it's different. I can't explain why, but it is."

She crouched down before he could argue, running her hands along the hardwood floor under the desk. "Let's find your wallet. I bet it fell out of your pocket. Those pants are so completely baggy, it's a wonder they haven't fallen right off your body."

"I'm sure we could arrange that," he mumbled as he

bent down beside her. At her glare, he said, "Kidding! Sheesh. But you know I'm right. I mean, about the surface dressing. Not the pants falling off. Not unless you—"

Her knuckles bumped something soft, and she stretched her fingers out to encircle cool leather. "Found it!"

"Really?"

She handed him the wallet, being careful not to let her fingers touch his, then stood up, relieved not to have to continue the conversation. She just couldn't go down that road with her life, so there was no point in discussing it. She had to think of him the way she had thought about Frankie the night she arrived in Juniper. As someone who couldn't help her, so she couldn't get attached, no matter how cute he might be.

Although Jake had a lot more going for him than Frankie. Not that she wanted to think about what Jake had going for him.

"See?" She gestured toward his clothes. "Baggy pants. Must've fallen out of your pocket."

"Thanks." He thumped the wallet against one thigh, then said, "Look, Seneca, about—"

"Let's discuss it another time, if you think we absolutely must. If I don't catch up to Drew and Claire right now, they're going to wonder what's going on, and then Claire will get more pissed off at me than she already is."

"All right. I need to get home and change into dry clothes, anyway. I told my dad I'd be back at the station in time to close up for him." He gave her a cryptic smile and tucked a strand of hair behind her ear. "To be continued, then?"

Seneca smiled back. She loved when guys touched her hair. Part of her was desperate to kiss him one more time, but she'd regret it, and so would he.

She'd had enough of making people feel bad today.

"Fine. To be continued."

She passed through the main lobby and turned into the hall leading to the cafeteria before it occurred to her he might have meant continuing the kissing part, not the discussion part.

*** seventeen ***

Claire slid her cafeteria tray onto an empty table close to one of the wall-mounted emergency lights. So much for the total relaxation she'd experienced during yoga class. It had lasted all of about twenty seconds once class ended, even though, like Cory, she loved thunderstorms. Plus, walking around with only the emergency lighting on was kind of fun.

Wondering whether or not Seneca would join them for dinner was not.

"I bet Seneca's going to flake out on us and go do something with Jake," she said to Drew once she'd taken a seat and they'd both peeled back the tops on their prepackaged salads and fruit cups.

She wanted to say something a lot more harsh, but Cory was right. Making the most of life meant doing the best you could in the present moment. For Claire that meant being a good Christian and not bashing Seneca. Too much.

"We'll see," Drew said after she swallowed a forkful of lettuce and shaved carrot. "I think she'll be here. I don't know what's up with the two of you, but she seemed upset by it. Like she wanted to talk to you about whatever it is and get past it."

"*She* wanted to get past it? That'd be just great for her. She's the one at fault here, not me."

Drew waved her hand in a gesture that said, *Out with it already.*

"She was flirting with Aaron and I saw her," Claire said. "That's it in a nutshell. I walked into the spa to warn them about the thunderstorm and Seneca was reaching over the desk"—she grabbed Drew's wrist, caressing it the way she'd seen Seneca do with Aaron—"just like this, giving Aaron a look that basically said, 'I'm all yours, baby. Take me here and now.' It was revolting. She has no conscience."

She let go of Drew and rolled her eyes. "I don't know why it surprised me. She's been curious about Aaron since the day she got to Juniper. For all I know, they've been out having a grand old time around town every night. She's certainly been out enough to have hooked up with him."

"So ask her what's going on," Drew said. "See what she says. Maybe it was just innocent flirting. You know she's like that. She checks out every single male when she enters a room, and they're always checking her out, too. It's like she has a magnet in her brain that instantly draws her to anything with testosterone. But"—Drew set down her fork and met Claire's gaze— "I have to ask why you really care. I know you and Aaron went out for a long time and that you probably had pretty strong feelings for him. But you two broke up. If he and Seneca have something going on, there's nothing you can do about it. Being mad at Seneca won't make it better. You need to live in the present, like Cory said."

"Easier said than done."

"Worth a try. If Aaron's the type of guy who'd go straight from you to Seneca without blinking, then flirt openly with her right in the building where he knows you work, is he the kind of guy you really want? You deserve a guy who likes you for *you*. A guy who treats you with the respect you deserve."

Claire twisted her fork in her salad, flipping the lettuce leaves around to spread the dressing. "I don't know if *he* was flirting with *her*. I only saw what Seneca did. And it's not like I couldn't get him back if I wanted to."

"Then why don't you?"

"It's complicated." How could she phrase this without making him sound like a jerk? "I changed a lot between when we saw each other over spring break and when he got here for the summer. And I kept some things from him that maybe I shouldn't have. I dumped all of it in his lap right when he got here, and it was a lot for him to deal with. He broke up with me when I stood my ground and refused to compromise. He's a good person, though."

Drew took a sip of her water. "Look, I'm sorry if I said something I shouldn't have about him, but—"

"It's okay. You're right. I have to wonder if he respects me anymore. We haven't talked. I'm not even sure if I *want* to talk, not unless . . . oh, I don't know." Claire swallowed hard. She could feel the tears welling in her eyes, so she took a deep breath to keep her emotions in check. Everything Drew said made sense, but it wasn't what she wanted to hear. She'd spent the last few weeks desperately hoping that Aaron would change his mind. That he'd accept her decision and that they could go back to the way their relationship was before they'd started having sex. Things had been great then. She'd hoped he could see that.

But now, for the first time, she realized with just as much certainty that it wasn't going to happen. And even though it was tempting to change her mind, that wasn't going to happen either.

She needed to do what was best for *her*, just like Todd

Mirelli advised when he came to the cabin earlier. Just like Drew was saying now.

"I need to let him go," she said. "I don't belong with Aaron. No matter how wonderful he is, no matter how much I love him, we don't belong together. We did in the past but we're on different paths toward the future. It's just that it hurts. A *lot*."

"It's probably going to hurt for a while," Drew said. "But don't blame Seneca, okay?"

The door to the cafeteria opened and both of them turned to look.

"Speaking of," Claire whispered.

"Hi. Sorry it took me so long."

"Hey, Seneca," Drew replied. "Jake find his wallet?"

"It was under the desk. Must've fallen out of his pocket. I told him it's those ugly-ass baggy pants he wears." She walked across the cafeteria to the counter and grabbed a tray before squinting at the selections. "Strange being the only ones in here, isn't it? Everyone else on staff has obviously eaten already, 'cause there's hardly anything left."

"The kitchen guys put the food out and went home early. We grabbed salads," Drew said, gesturing toward where they were stacked at the end of the counter. "There are some fruit cups in the minifridge. They're hard to see, but I felt a couple more in there toward the front left when I got mine."

"Thanks." Once her tray was full, Seneca walked to the table and scooted in right across from Claire.

Of course.

Seneca smiled at Claire, then looked sideways at Drew. "So, what'd you guys think of Goddess Yoga?"

Drew swallowed a bite of salad. "I actually liked it. It was a little woo-woo for me, with all that talk about the Three Goddesses or Three Fates or whoever—I don't give a rip what ancient Hindu and Roman cultures believed—but it wasn't too over-the-top. And my muscles feel like I've gotten a great workout."

"Ankle's okay?"

"Ankle's great."

A wave of guilt washed over Claire. How could she not have thought about Drew's ankle? Would she ever learn to think of other people first? "I'm sorry, Drew! I meant to ask how you were feeling when we got out of class."

"Claire, I'm *fine*. I swear, you're critical of yourself when you really shouldn't be. Keep doing that and it'll screw you up."

Claire gave Drew a sheepish smile. "I'll try to keep that in mind."

"Cory got me thinking," Seneca said, her gaze focused

directly on Claire in a way that made Claire want to squirm. "You know, with all her talk about making the most of the present. The thing is, you guys are my present, and I've been a lousy roommate." She turned to Drew. "I was nasty to you the first couple days we were here. You're right—I was a total space hog, and I'm sorry. I should have apologized a long time ago."

Drew looked surprised for a moment, then she shrugged. "No problem. Now, if you'd actually thrown my shoes out the window, it'd take me longer to accept your apology. And for the record, I'm sorry I dumped your stuff all over your bed. And that I left my dumbbells where you could trip on them."

"No, I deserved it. I guess I'm not used to living with anyone but my mom. Plus, we had a housekeeper until recently, so when I had too much stuff on the bathroom counter, it got cleaned up. And I never had to watch out for anyone else's things." Seneca made a face. "I guess, in a way, it was good for me that you did it."

Claire kept on eating her fruit salad, waiting for Seneca to say something to her. It was all fine and dandy that Drew and Seneca were willing to forgive and forget, but she wasn't there yet. Grabbing someone's shoes and grabbing their boyfriend—or ex-boyfriend—were entirely different things.

Even if she and Aaron weren't getting back together.

Plus, girls like Seneca were the type who'd say whatever it took to save their own tail in a scrape. Claire had done the same thing herself. She'd lied to her school friends to get out of plans when Aaron was in town and she'd wanted to spend more time with him. She'd certainly lied to her parents and friends about her moodiness after finding out she was pregnant. She'd even lied to her mom the night she miscarried, convincing Mom that she was in the bathroom so long because she'd eaten something that didn't agree with her. She'd faked embarrassment, then took the Pepto-Bismol Mom offered, because she knew it'd make Mom feel like she'd done her parenting duty.

Claire had done it to save her own tail.

"And, Claire, I owe you an even bigger apology."

Claire stabbed a strawberry slice with her fork, then popped it in her mouth, waiting.

"I didn't like Drew when I first got here—sorry, Drew—but Claire, I've liked you from day one."

"You just liked my Tory Burch top." The one Aaron bought for her.

"Of course I liked it. It's gorgeous on you. But I liked you, too. You didn't yell at me in the food line when I was being obnoxious—even though the food choices were horrid and I still think I had a right to complain—and you didn't get upset with me when I left you only one drawer in our bedroom dresser." She glanced at Drew. "I did give her a second drawer after you yelled at me, though."

"I noticed." Drew replied. "Of course, if you hadn't, I'd have moved your stuff for you."

Seneca and Drew laughed, but guilt gnawed at Claire. She'd tried to ditch Seneca after talking to her in the food line—precisely because she was afraid she might like Seneca too much and might be tempted to follow Seneca out to the clubs where she'd been hanging out with Aaron during his vacations, getting to know the Hollywood crowd, getting to party with them.

Ignoring what God wanted for her.

Seneca focused on Claire again. "The thing is, I never should have pestered you about Aaron. And I shouldn't have flirted with him today in the spa. I have zero interest— truly, zero interest—in going out with the guy. And I wanted you to know that. Even if I did, I'd never steal someone else's boyfriend, no matter what."

"So why all the questions, then? You've been asking me about him nearly every day for three weeks. You had to have a reason."

Seneca flicked her napkin open and dropped it on her lap, but Claire could tell she wasn't paying attention to the napkin at all.

"It's just, well, Aaron's dad is a really big deal in Hollywood. I mean, a *really* big deal. Not quite on par with Steven Spielberg or Ron Howard, but close. And I wanted to make a connection with his dad because my mom's an actress, and no matter how talented you are or how many awards you've won, you can always use a positive connection with a guy like Elliott Grey."

"You're saying you were flirting with my boyfriend to help your *mom*?" Her superfamous, superactress mom couldn't possibly need help. But then again, hadn't Todd said that Dahlia and Violet were telling everyone that Jacqueline Billeray's career was in the toilet? She herself had seen Seneca IM-ing her mom and gotten the feeling something heavy was being discussed.

Could the Koss sisters have known—for once—what they were talking about?

But Seneca was nodding, like she thought she'd finally gotten through to Claire. "Exactly. It's an everyday thing to schmooze like that in L.A., but I should have reined it in here in Juniper, especially because—even though you didn't say so—I was starting to get the feeling you didn't want me to talk to him. If I hurt your feelings, I'm sorry."

Claire studied Seneca's face. Seneca *did* seem sorry. But there was always the chance she was as good an actress as her mother and was just saying what she knew Claire wanted to hear.

"And," Seneca added, "I had no clue, *none*, that the two of you might be having problems. Not until I saw how you reacted to seeing each other in the spa. I could tell the second you guys looked at each other that you were either in a fight or broken up. If I'd known, I wouldn't have acted the way I did."

"Wait, are you blaming me for not telling you?"

"Of course not!" Seneca threaded her fingers through her hair, pulling it away from her face. Whether the action was out of embarrassment or because she was trying to hide something, Claire couldn't tell. "I was the one who screwed up here. Totally my bad."

Something still didn't feel quite right. Claire played with her fruit cup for a moment, trying to get a read on Seneca. She seemed desperate to be forgiven, but the more anxious Seneca looked while waiting for Claire to say everything was all right, the more questions Claire had.

"So," Claire began, "you figured out pretty quickly after you got here that my boyfriend happens to be the son of Elliott Grey. But there are dozens of people who are worth schmoozing in Juniper at this time of year. People who are just as A-list as Elliott Grey. Why chase him so hard?"

"It's a complex thing," Seneca replied. "I'm sure—"

"I'm smart," Claire replied. "If you explain it, I'll be able to figure it out."

"Well . . ." Seneca glanced around, like she was afraid someone would overhear them. "You guys promise to keep this to yourselves? I mean, *really* keep it to yourselves?"

Drew shrugged. Claire just waved for Seneca to spit it out. She wasn't making any promises until she heard Seneca's explanation.

And maybe not even then.

❖ EIGHTEEN *❖*

Seneca bit her lip. How could she change the subject yet still convince Claire that she felt awful about what happened?

After a few seconds of trying to come up with something to say, something that might distract Claire, she knew she couldn't. Claire needed to know.

Seneca pushed her tray away and said, "I've been coming to Juniper every summer since I was in, I dunno, seventh or eighth grade. I know most of those A-list people and they know me. I've gone to their pool parties and to all the 'in' places at night. But those people also know Axel Randolph."

Drew frowned. "Who's he?"

"A producer. His name's not as well known outside Hollywood and Juniper as Elliott Grey's, because Elliott is also a director. He's won awards, gotten a lot of publicity. But Axel's just as powerful as Mr. Grey. Plus he's loaded, he knows *everyone*, and"—she took a deep breath—"Axel was my mom's boyfriend. I was here in Juniper the last few summers because my mom and I were living with Axel. He has a second home here and always stays in Juniper during the summer."

"I know which house is his," Claire said. "I heard he was a producer, but that's it."

Seneca knew her surprise showed on her face. "How can you not know who he is?" And that he'd lived with her mom?

Claire gave a one-shouldered shrug. "My family sells sporting goods. I didn't really know anyone from the whole Hollywood, megarich summer crowd that well until I started seeing Aaron. I grew up hanging out with the year-round people."

Claire took a sip of her drink, then added, "And even then, I was just hanging out with other teenagers. Not people my parents' age, like Axel Randolph."

"So what happened with your mom and this Axel guy?" Drew asked. "Must've been nasty."

"He was a jerk." Understatement of the century. "Mom and I moved out of Axel's house over the Fourth of July weekend, right in the middle of the summer, so everyone in town heard about it. There was even a paragraph about it in *People*: 'Longtime couple Jacqueline Billeray and multimillionaire producer Axel Randolph have split. Sources in Juniper, Colorado, where Randolph and Billeray keep a summer residence, say Billeray and her sixteen-year-old daughter, Seneca, have moved out. The Academy Award–winning actress's belongings were seen being loaded onto a moving van over the holiday weekend. A spokesperson for Randolph says the presence of the van was a private matter but refused to elaborate further. Billeray's publicist had no comment. Billeray is said to be in seclusion at her Beverly Hills home.'"

"Ouch," Drew murmured.

"No kidding. Can you tell I read that paragraph only a few dozen times?" She shook her head. "The really bad part, though, is that since then—and this is the part that has to be completely between us—my mom hasn't gotten a single job. *Nothing*."

"Wow," Claire said.

"The whole time she was with Axel, he refused to let her do any work that required travel. So it's all been guest spots and occasional voiceover work. Not much to build her resume. But that's not the worst of it."

"How so?" Claire asked.

"We don't know for sure, but both of us think Axel bad-mouthed Mom to his friends, even if he was refusing to comment about her in public. So now even if people want to work with my mom, no one is going to risk pissing off Axel by casting her in one of their projects. There are a zillion other actresses dying to get work, so why not hire one of them, you know?"

"But you thought Elliott Grey might help her if you got to know the family?"

Seneca nodded. "I took the job here in Juniper because Mom wanted me to earn my own spending money, but also because I was hoping I could schmooze the summer people here in Juniper while my mom kept trying to network and get auditions back at home. The first night I was here, though, I figured out how bad my mom's situation was."

"What do you mean?" Drew asked.

"I didn't realize that people around here see her as a joke. It freaked me out." Even in the dim lighting, she was certain they could see her face flush as she told them about the first night she'd come to town—about the Koss sisters, the cell phone, everything. "I knew if *they* were willing to treat me like dirt, pretty much anyone who was friends with Axel—or who was plugged into Juniper's rumor mill—would do the same thing."

"So you kept asking me about Aaron, since his family's fairly new in town."

Seneca nodded. "When I realized who his dad had to be, I got this feeling like this whole summer was meant to be. After that evening with Dahlia and Violet, I thought . . . I dunno . . . like I'd been given another chance or something. Elliott Grey directs serious films—the kind my mom generally does—so if he hired her, it'd be a good fit. And even if he didn't, his production company backs lots of projects. Projects where he could toss out my mom's name as a possible lead. I built up the opportunity in my head, and I went totally overboard."

She reached across the table and put her hand over Claire's. "Claire, I'm so, so sorry. I should have told you at the beginning, but I was afraid to tell anyone about my mom's situation. I'm *still* afraid to tell anyone. Reputation in the film business can be a self-fulfilling prophecy. If you look desirable, then people want to cast you. If you look like a loser who's desperate for a job, no one will touch you, talent or not. So I didn't want anyone to know how bad things had gotten. I wanted everyone to think my mom was doing fabulously."

Seneca sat back, letting go of Claire's hand. She tried to control her voice, but it cracked as she said, "All Cory's talk about living in the present got me thinking about how mean I've acted all summer. I've been a shallow, self-absorbed idiot."

As she looked from Claire to Drew and back to Claire, she knew she'd done the right thing in telling them. She laughed to herself, then said, "As insane as this sounds, you guys are probably the closest thing to friends I have right now. I don't want to mess that up. I want friends who are actually my *friends*, not because I'm schmoozing them or because they think it's cool to say they've met Jacqueline Billeray's daughter."

Claire closed her eyes. Seneca's heart dropped. But when Claire opened her eyes, she was smiling. "Maybe, if you'll forgive me for calling you what I did back in the spa, I can forgive you. And we can start all over again."

"Really?"

"Ooh, ooh!" Drew's eyes filled with mischief. "What terrible thing did our resident Bible-thumper call you, Seneca? A meanie? A jerk?"

"Hey, don't call me a Bible-thumper! I've never thumped a Bible against anything or anyone in my life."

"She called me a bitch."

"Claire?" Drew's jaw dropped. "*This* Claire used *that* word? It's not in her vocabulary!"

"I promise you, it's in her vocabulary." Seneca grinned at Claire. "And I deserved it."

"Are you kidding me?" Drew said.

"You'd be surprised what's in my vocabulary. But I'm trying to get that stuff out," Claire told them. She was quiet for a moment, then said, "Seneca, are you *positive* you're not interested in Aaron? Because, if you are, I understand. Cory got me thinking, too. Aaron is in my past. I need to let go of him. I need to let go of everything that happened when we were together."

"I'm not interested in him," Seneca said.

"It's okay if you are."

"I'm not, already! I'm interested in someone else."

Why did she say that?

Covering, Seneca added, "It's not something that's going to work out, so no biggie. My point is that I'm *not* interested in Aaron. All right?"

"You're interested in someone—" Drew's eyes widened. "No way. No *way*!"

Seneca glared at Drew, hoping she'd shut up, but Claire was already asking, "What? Who?"

"It's Jake, isn't it?" Drew asked. "You like Jake! But you think he's not your type, so you don't want to admit it either."

Seneca shot back, "And you like Rob, Miss Know-It-All. But for some reason, you don't want to admit it, either."

Claire turned to Drew. "You did avoid Rob at lunch

today. Did something happen with you guys? Like, when you hurt your ankle? Or is it *because* of the ankle? Is he upset that you can't go running with—"

"We're not going there," Drew said, waving her off. "We're talking about Seneca and Jake."

"There's nothing to talk about," Seneca insisted. Not that it'd get Drew to shut up. Drew didn't want the attention on what was—or wasn't—happening with Rob any more than Seneca wanted it on herself and Jake.

"I don't know Jake that well," Claire said. "He's a year older than me, so we've never been in the same classes. But everyone says he's a nice guy. And I don't think he's seeing anyone else. So why not—"

"I don't think it'd work, so there's no point in discussing it," Seneca interrupted. Why, why, why had she opened her big, fat mouth? Probably because, other than trying to make things right between her and Claire, Jake was all she'd been able to think about for days. She was bound to have screwed up and mentioned him sometime. And now that they'd kissed . . .

"Something happened when you were helping him look for his wallet, didn't it?" Drew asked. "Or earlier today?"

Seneca wrapped her napkin around her fingers. Now that they knew, she may as well let it all out and get their advice. "He kissed me."

"And?"

"Rocked my world. But it can't happen! He lives here, I'm in California—"

"Wasn't a problem for me and Aaron," Claire argued. "We had issues or we wouldn't be broken up right now, but distance wasn't one of them. You can work around that."

"It's more than that. His dad runs a gas station and his mom sells souvenirs. My mom is . . ." She let the thought trail off. She'd probably offended them both with her rich-kid views. But she knew she was right. "We just come from different worlds."

"Seneca, if you go for it, what's the worst that can happen?" Claire asked.

"He decides I'm shallow. He decides I'm stupid."

He breaks my heart.

"You guys have spent a lot of time together in the spa. If he kissed you, I bet he doesn't think those things," Claire said. "Is it that *you* don't want to be seen with *him*?"

"I don't know." Seneca continued to play with the napkin in her lap. "Maybe."

The lights flickered, then came back on, bathing the cafeteria in light.

"When did he kiss you?" Claire asked, ignoring the

lights. "Just now, when you were helping him find his wallet?"

Seneca nodded.

"And you came in here after us?" Claire persisted.

"I needed to apologize to you both. And I was scared out of my mind by Jake."

"You want to kiss him again?"

"Claire! How do I know?" She wadded up her napkin and tossed it onto her tray. She couldn't bear to look at either one of them, so she focused her attention on the napkin. "Okay, yes, I'd love to. But I told him it wouldn't work. I told him we were from different worlds and that I'd end up hurting his feelings. He left and went back to the gas station to close up for his dad."

"I've only talked to the guy once or twice," Drew commented. "He sat by me once at lunch last week, though, and from what I could tell, he deserves more credit than that."

Seneca snapped her gaze to Drew. "That's what *he* said. That I don't give him enough credit. Right now he probably figures he gave me too much. How could I have said something so mean to him?"

Claire glanced at Drew, smiled, then bent down to get something out of her gym bag. She slid a set of car keys across the table.

"What are these for?" Seneca asked.

"You warmed up your apology skills on us. Now I think you should go apologize to Jake." Claire pointed in the direction of the employee parking lot. "Black Lexus, third spot over from the path. All yours. Do you know how to get to his dad's gas station?"

When Seneca shook her head, Claire gave her directions.

Seneca put her hand over the key ring, rubbing her thumb along a miniature Colorado license plate that read CLAIRE.

She shouldn't do this. It was raining. He was working. He could get mad at her.

Or, worst of all, he might've decided she was right, that she wasn't any good for him.

"Normally, the last thing I'd tell someone is to chase down a guy," Drew said quietly. "But maybe—"

"Just do it," Claire interrupted.

Seneca opened her mouth to protest, then closed it. Really, would it be so bad to just go for it with Jake? Like Claire said, what's the worst that could happen?

She had to take the chance. And no way did she want to make an apology tomorrow at work with Kelsey hanging around.

"Claire, thanks for the car. You're the best."

Claire's grin was the biggest Seneca had ever seen from her. "It's the least I can do for a friend. Go! We'll get your tray."

Seneca tightened her grip on the keys and pushed back from the table. She started to stand, but the sight of Drew gathering up their trays stopped her.

"I'll tell you what. I'll go for it with Jake if Drew goes for it with Rob."

Drew sagged against the table, then pretended to beat her head against it. "Seneca, just *go*. Your situation and mine are completely different."

Seneca sat back down and stared at Drew.

"Tell us what's up with Rob, please?" Claire asked in a much nicer voice than Seneca would have used. "Otherwise, we're never going to get rid of her."

"Yeah, because I'll start telling her how stupid it is to get dependent on a guy, and how I don't want to go there."

"'Dependent on' and 'attracted to' are totally different things," Seneca said.

"Okay, fine," Drew said when Claire and Seneca made it clear they weren't going to budge. Drew shoved the stacked trays off to the side, then rested her elbows on the table. "I didn't tell you guys the whole story with my ankle and how I hurt it. I was running the Rocky Ridge trail and stopped hard because I saw a bear."

"A bear?" Claire's eyes looked like they were going to pop out of her head. "There aren't that many around here, and even then, they try to avoid humans. I hope you reported it!"

"Was it close to you?" Seneca asked. "I think I'd have peed my pants!"

"I reported it. And, Seneca, for your info, I almost did pee my pants. It was scratching itself on a tree on the trail right in front of me. Rob was behind me and saw the whole thing when I hurt myself. The bear ran off, but"—Drew made a face—"the thing scared me so much I lost my lunch. Right in front of Rob."

"Ewww," Seneca said, then added quickly, "but those things happen. No biggie."

Claire's skeptical look mirrored the way Seneca felt. "You're avoiding Rob because you barfed in front of him? It's not like you got drunk or did something stupid. Or that you barfed *on* him. It's not worth being embarrassed about."

"Did something else happen?" Seneca asked.

"Nothing I want to talk about."

"You sure you didn't pee your pants?"

"I did *not* pee my pants! I just said something to Rob that I shouldn't have. It's personal. All right?" The look on Drew's face made it clear her decision was final.

Seneca reached over and put her hand on Drew's arm. "Whatever you said to him—and I understand if it's something you don't want to talk about—do you think he won't like you because of it? Or that it makes you look less than invincible or something? Because I know that's how you portray yourself—like you're invincible, like nothing can hurt you, like you're tough and strong and you're going to have your name engraved on plaques with running records—but I bet Rob doesn't care about that. He's certainly not going to think you're dependent on him."

"She's right," Claire added. "He cares about you or he wouldn't have come to the cabin to see how you're doing. But that doesn't equal dependence."

Drew shook off Seneca's hand. "You guys are going all Dr. Phil on me. Stop. I'm *fine*. The Rob thing is not a big deal."

"Promise you'll talk to him and clear it up?" Seneca prodded. "Because I think you two would be great together, and it'd be silly to—"

Drew rolled her eyes as only Drew could. "If I promise, will you go see Jake already?"

Seneca grabbed Drew's hand and shook it before Drew could protest. "Deal! I'm outta here."

She stood and smoothed her top. "Do I look okay?"

"You're fine. And he's not going to care," Claire said. "Go!"

Seneca grinned. "You guys are way better friends to me than Dahlia and Violet Koss could ever be."

Claire stood, then picked up the trays Drew had stacked. "And it's terrible of me to say it, but I'm starting to realize that you two will be better friends to me than Amanda and Delia could ever be. They make assumptions about me because of things I did in the past, even though I've done everything possible to change their minds. With you guys I've never had to do that. You just accept me for who I am, even if you don't always agree with me."

"Ditto," Drew added, standing up and looping her backpack over her shoulder. "Though I can't say I have any other friends to compare you to. At this moment you guys are it for me. So, Seneca, get outta here before I get emotional, because emotional is *not* a good look for me. I hate it."

Seneca leaned over to give Drew a quickie hug, thanked Claire, then turned and walked out of the cafeteria, keys in hand.

Once the door shut behind her and she was in the hallway, out of sight of Drew and Claire, she started to jog.

NINETEEN

Seneca guided Claire's Lexus past a large rack of wind-shield wiper fluid, then around the side of the Camarillo Street Exxon into an empty spot beside the Dumpster. The power outage had prevented Jake from seeing her fully at the spa, but the lights were blazing inside the Exxon. He was going to get an up-close look at her under the fluorescents.

She put on the emergency brake, unbuckled, then stretched to look in the rearview mirror.

Damn. She should have gone to the cabin first.

It was obvious, even in the car mirror, that she'd been exercising, and not just because she wore no makeup—not even her fave Chanel tinted moisturizer. Her once-pristine ponytail had come loose from all those repetitions of downward dog and, worse, getting soaked running from the lodge to Claire's car had made all that loose hair stringy.

She smoothed her hands over her hair, then looked out the driver's-side window. Though it had slowed to a drizzle, the rain obscured her view. But she knew the lines of a Mercedes well enough to identify the lone vehicle pulling out of the self-service lane. An instant wave of regret hit her. Claire was great about giving her the Lexus, but her Mercedes had been her baby. It wasn't the same to drive someone else's car.

She rested her head against the steering wheel and counted to ten. Her Mercedes was gone, never to return. She had to learn to live with it. To quit feeling like she *deserved* a Mercedes, just because.

A Toyota eased into the self-service lane. An older man got out with an umbrella, punched the buttons on the pump so he could use his credit card, then opened the gas cap on his car.

A voice—Jake's?—came over an intercom stating that his credit card was approved, then it clicked out. Otherwise, the station was quiet. No cars on the road, nothing to delay her.

But she couldn't move.

"You can do this," she muttered. So she'd screwed things up with Jake. Hollywood loved a comeback, right? She closed her eyes for one long, deep breath, then told herself again, "You can do this. Think

Vanessa Williams. John Travolta. Kate Moss."

Why not Seneca Billeray?

She pulled the keys from the ignition and got out, sprinted to the glass door, then yanked it open and hurried inside.

There wasn't anyone at the register.

She glanced around. Someone had to be here. She walked along the aisles, past displays of granola bars and sunflower seeds and the spinning rack of tacky sunglasses before finally spotting Jake's familiar form at the back of the store, loading sodas into one of the refrigerator cases with the same ease he stocked towels at the spa.

As she approached he said, "I'll be at the register in just a sec," then spun around before she could answer. Surprise registered on his face. "Seneca."

The refrigerator door shut behind him with a thud.

"Hey, Jake."

"I thought you were someone coming in to buy snacks." He pushed his glasses up and his gaze locked with hers. Neither of them moved. He'd changed into loose jeans and a fresh T-shirt emblazoned with the station's logo.

His hair was still damp and in its usual messy state, but he looked clean. He looked confident. He looked *incredible*.

He jammed his hands into his front pockets, rocked back on his heels, and smiled. "Now, what would bring Hollywood It Girl Seneca Billeray into an Exxon station in Juniper, Colorado? Is she doing film research for her superstar mother? Perhaps she's decided to go on the Convenience Store Diet, which is rumored to be the latest craze on the West Coast. Twinkies for breakfast, coffee and a Nutri-Grain bar for lunch, a Diet Coke for dinner, and it's only a thousand calories! Or maybe she—"

"I came to see you, you moron." How was it that even when she felt so tense she wanted to pull a Drew move and hurl right in front of him, he managed to make her laugh?

"Hmmmm." He took a few steps toward her. "Not sure how *The National Enquirer* would spin that one. Lemme see . . . maybe the headline would read something like, 'Oscar Winner's Daughter Caught in Convenience Mart with—'"

"A guy she doesn't deserve." Her throat seized up on the last word. Just looking at him, seeing him at the end of the aisle, made her realize how much she wanted him. How wonderful and interesting a person he was.

And how she really hadn't given him enough credit.

Jake stopped walking. "Didn't we go over this at the spa? You said it wouldn't work. That we come from different places and I don't understand how you live. All that stuff."

"It might not work." He might not even be interested anymore. Or they might get a day or a week or a month down the road and decide they had nothing in common. "But I've been thinking about it. Maybe we could try, if you'd be willing to overlook my shallow tendencies."

"What do you think I do at the spa desk all day long?"

He meant it as a joke, but Seneca didn't laugh. She took a hesitant step forward. "What you see there is *nothing*. I may kiss up to the clients, but that actually has a purpose. If you're around me for any length of time, I guarantee you're going to hear me whine about not having the latest Balenciaga bag in more than one color. Most people would kill to have the money just one of those purses cost so they could afford to pay their rent. But do I think of that when I whine? No. And that's just for starters."

"You're not that bad."

"Yes, I am." And that was the truth. "I lie in bed at night picturing purses and shoes I simply *must* have. And it's not always like you said before, that I want those things because it'll help my mom and make it look like we belong in a certain crowd. I want them for *me*. I want to go on vacations to St. Bart's so I can lie on the beach and have someone else clean up after me. I want expensive jewelry that I'll maybe wear a couple times, then won't wear again because people have seen it already. I want the fanciest makeup and hair products because even if all the ingredients are the same as in something I can grab off the shelf here in your gas station, I like the *name*. I'm trying to get better, but right now, that's who I am."

Jake rocked forward, then back again, his hands still in his pockets. "That's human nature. We all want that kind of life, Seneca. At least on some days we do. But what's important is who we are on the inside. How we treat other people. How we get along with each other."

"I suck at that."

"Not as much as you think. We get along great at work. You make me laugh. You treat people with respect. And even if you want that Balla-whatever purse, you don't think less of someone else if they don't have one."

Seneca closed the gap between them and gave his shoulder a playful shove. "I make you laugh? I'm not funny. You're the one who's funny, with your little entertainment reports and your jokes about Kelsey and the spa clients. I'm just . . . well, there's a difference between being someone you can laugh at and someone you can laugh with. And I think you laugh at me more than you laugh with me."

"Ditto. I know you laugh with me, but you laugh *at* my clothing choices. You laugh at the fact I have hair on my toes and make no secret of the fact you're grossed out by it. And you laugh at the fact I don't like Jimmy Buffett."

She couldn't help the grin spreading across her face. "Someone *should* laugh at your clothing choices and your hairy toes. And your musical taste."

"You're as good a candidate as anyone." He leaned down so his face was only a few inches from hers, definitely within kissing range.

It was possibly the most romantic moment of her life, and she was in the middle of an Exxon station candy aisle.

"What do you think of Prince?" he whispered.

"Prince?"

"You know, Prince. 'When Doves Cry,' 'Purple Rain'?"

"Oh, that Prince. I like Prince."

"Me too." He leaned his forehead against hers, and she could feel his smile as much as she could see it. "You know his song 'Kiss'? Where he says you don't have to be rich to be my girl?"

"Or cool to rule my world, or something like that?"

"That's the song." His hands slid around her waist, and he said, "'I just want your extra time, and your—'"

He gave her the softest, sweetest kiss, then jerked and took a step away from her.

The sick feeling returned to her stomach. Did she

have salad dressing breath or something? "Um—"

"Sorry. Just remembered that there are security cameras. Not sure I want my dad reviewing the tape, you know?"

"Oh."

"But the station closes in ten minutes. And I have no plans whatsoever."

She ventured, "Maybe we can go for a drive? You know, just go around town, make it a leisurely thing?" Find a spot where they could finish what they'd started.

A bell rang at the front of the shop. He glanced toward the counter, then back to her. A wide grin spread across his face. "Definitely."

"I can wait in my car if that's—"

"Actually, would you mind sticking those sodas in the fridge for me while I ring up this customer? I'll be able to get out of here faster if everything is stocked."

"Sure."

He gave her a fast, promising kiss, then turned and walked toward the counter. She went to the refrigerator, studying which sodas occupied each of the racks, then pulled open the glass door and started sliding plastic bottles of Diet Pepsi into the empty slot next to the regular Pepsi bottles.

Ten minutes. She could handle waiting ten minutes.

She grinned to herself as she reached down to grab the necks of a few more bottles. She could hear female voices at the front of the store but couldn't pick out the words. Sounded like teenagers picking up last-minute essentials before going out for the night.

Curious about who it could be, she glanced in their direction as she slid another Diet Pepsi into place.

She could just see the top of a platinum blonde head over the aisles. A dark-haired male was close to the blonde. When he turned, Seneca caught sight of his face as he reached for a box of Cheez-Its.

Frankie. The guy from The Final Run. Which meant the platinum blonde whose head was so close to his had to be Dahlia's, since the girl was too tall to be Violet.

Seneca rolled her eyes as she slid another Diet Pepsi into its slot. All that cigarette smoking had probably stunted Violet's growth.

"Oh, my. What have we here?"

Seneca spun around to see Violet standing in the aisle behind her. "Hi, Violet. What's up?"

"We're heading to Tabby's Bar with Frankie. You gonna be there later? I keep hearing that you're out and about but we never seem to catch you lately." She took a long, slow look up and down Seneca's outfit. "You just come from a gym or something? You look like hell."

"Thanks, Violet. Always appreciate a compliment."

"Huh?"

Seneca ignored her. The girl was beyond dense.

"You'd be better off drinking water than that carbonated, artificially flavored stuff," Violet said as she strode to the refrigerator compartment next to Seneca's and grabbed a bottle of Evian. "I hope you're going to change before you go out tonight. Or are you not going out? You must get so tired, working at King's Crown like slave labor."

"It's not slave labor. I actually like it."

Violet raised an eyebrow. "Seriously?"

"Seriously." Seneca bent down to grab two more Diet Pepsis and slide them into their slot. "I get to take classes at the spa—I took one tonight called Goddess Yoga—and I've met lots of fabulous people."

Seneca got a jolt of satisfaction at the shocked—and jealous—look that passed over Violet's face. But then Violet stepped back and put a hand on her Calvin Klein—clad hip. "What are you doing with those Cokes?"

Pepsis, you moron. "Loading 'em in."

"Duh. I see that. So, like, what are you doing? Are you going to steal some?"

"Hey, Violet!" Dahlia's voice carried over the aisles.

"Move your ass if you want me to pay for your water. The guy up here says it's closing time. You want me to grab you a pack of Marlboro Lights?"

"Tell him to wait a sec," she called back, then said to Seneca, "Geez, freakin' gas station guy. You'd think he'd know a little bit about service."

"He knows plenty, Violet. He happens to be really nice."

Violet frowned, but only for a few seconds. Then Seneca swore the blonde's eyes might bug right out of her head. "Oh, gawd. Seneca Billeray, are you doin' the gas man?"

She laughed at her own question, then yelled in the direction of the front counter, "Hey, Dahlia, guess who's got the hots for the gas guy!"

Seneca swore to herself as Dahlia popped around the end of the aisle and saw her at the refrigerator door. She looked Seneca over, then laughed.

"Stephanie!" Frankie was right behind Dahlia. At the sight of Seneca he dropped his hand from Dahlia's waist. "Long time no see, baby!"

Seneca didn't bother to correct him about her name this time. Drunken idiot. Maybe Dahlia and Violet had done her a favor that first night she'd come into town, getting her away from him.

She glanced at Violet. "You should pay for your Evian. The cash register's on an electronic control; he can't ring you out after the station closes. Prevents theft, you know?"

Violet's eyes held a question, but she turned and walked to the cash register without asking it. Violet could've cared less about the Evian, Seneca was sure, but if she ran out of cigarettes, she'd go insane. Dahlia and Frankie looked at each other, then trailed after Violet.

They giggled their way out the door a few minutes later, then Seneca heard the purr of Violet's BMW as it pulled away. There was a clanking sound as Jake locked the glass doors behind them.

And good riddance.

The lights that illuminated the area around the gas pumps flickered out. For the next few minutes she slid the sodas into their slots, listening to Jake whistle as he secured the station.

As she took the last Pepsi from the crate and put it in its slot he came to stand beside her. "There's no electronic whatever-you-said on the register."

"Got them out of here, didn't it?"

He brushed against her as he bent to pick up the

empty crate that'd been holding the sodas. "Come on, follow me out the back."

"Are you done with everything you need to do?"

"Yep. I'd already cashed out when they got here, so I just had to lock up and wipe down the counter by the fountain drinks. I'll tell my dad to ring through their sale in the morning."

He led her past the self-serve coffee bar and through a door at the rear of the store, then past a small office stacked high with files. He opened another, heavier door and stuck his hand outside.

"Rain's picked up again."

"I'm already soaked, so no biggie," Seneca said. "You want to take my car or yours?"

He gave her a smile that made her giddy. He let go of the open door so it swung shut, leaving them enclosed in the rear hallway. "How 'bout we stay in here, just until the rain stops? Then we can go for a drive. Just wander wherever we feel like."

She reached toward him, and when her knuckles grazed his, he spread his fingers to interlace them with hers. "You mean we should see what there is to see, take things slow?"

"That's the whole point of a leisurely drive, isn't it?"

he whispered. "Go wherever the road takes you."

"Could be a while before the rain lets up," she said, leaning forward to kiss him. "But I like your plan."

Four hours later, she kissed Jake good-bye on the cabin's front porch, then slipped inside. Drew and Claire had left the lamp on next to the couch. Seneca grinned.

Big difference from the day Drew had left her dumbbells in front of the stairs.

She tiptoed across the room and clicked off the lamp, then eased her way up the stairs.

After she'd washed her face and changed into a T-shirt, she climbed into bed.

This had to be the best night of her life. How could she ever have sat with Frankie at The Final Run and imagined *that* was where she belonged?

This was where she belonged.

"So, how'd it go?" Drew whispered from across the room.

"Fabulous," she whispered back.

"Details!" Claire said, sitting up and clicking on her bedside lamp. "We need details."

Seneca hugged her pillow to her. "Well, first I got—" she paused. "Nope, I take that back. I'm not going to tell you."

"What?" Drew sat up. "That's totally uncool! You have to tell us *something*."

"I will." Seneca grinned, then rolled so she was facing away from them. "After Drew talks to Rob."

"Totally uncool is right," Claire muttered. "Drew, tomorrow you're talking to Rob."

✳ ✳ ✳ TWENTY ✳ ✳ ✳

"So, are you going to give us the details on last night?" Claire asked Seneca as they walked up the path to the main lodge with Drew. "Should I call Kelsey to the lobby on some errand so you and Jake can have alone time?"

"Uh-uh, not telling," Seneca said, waving a finger in Drew's direction. So much for hoping Seneca would forget.

"Guess you'd better talk to Rob," Claire said. "If you don't, I'm going to invite him to the cabin and lock the two of you in there."

"You do, and I'm going to ask for new roomies," Drew grumbled. "Some who'll split the cost of my Edensoy or who'll go to the gym with me in the morning to lift."

It felt good to know it was an empty threat and that Seneca and Claire knew it. Giggling with them last night after Seneca got home felt wonderful. Like she was making new friends for the first time in ages. Friends who wouldn't give her pathetic, babying looks because of what happened to her dad.

Of course, they didn't know about Dad. But maybe after they got to be better friends, when they realized she wasn't that pathetic, she could tell them about it. By that point, maybe discussing it wouldn't cause her to fall apart the way she did with Rob.

"You'll have a hard time," Claire said. "No one else on Earth can possibly stand that boxed soy milk. Ugh. You're stuck with us, and we're going to keep nagging you."

Drew gave Claire a lighthearted smack on the arm. "I'll talk to him, all right? But I swear, it's not that big a deal. I'm not interested in him the way Seneca is interested in Jake. This is different. Rob and I are just friends."

And if she were smart, she'd make absolutely sure it stayed that way.

She waved good-bye to Seneca and Claire as they reached the back door of the lodge. Seneca bounced off through the lobby in the direction of the spa—obviously happy to be seeing Jake—and Claire headed for the information desk. Drew walked, though still with a limp, down the hallway leading to the kitchen and another day of doing whatever scut work the regular kitchen guys needed her to do.

She couldn't wait for her ankle to heal. Another week, maybe, and she could try leading one of the easier hikes. Anything to get outdoors. Though that'd mean being where she could run into Rob at any time.

He might not have done anything flirty when they were up on the mountain—when he'd kissed her on top of the head, it'd been more comforting than romantic—but she still hadn't forgotten how he'd trapped her foot under the table that first day in the cafeteria.

And she remembered how dangerous it'd felt. Like something she could get used to and rely on to make her feel good when she was down. She never, ever wanted to rely on anyone to keep her in a happy mental state the way most girls seemed to rely on their boyfriends. She'd felt idiotic enough dumping on Rob once. The girls she knew with boyfriends seemed compelled to dump on them all the frickin' time.

No way did she want to become one of *those* girls.

Maybe that was why Mom was as whacked-out as she was. Maybe she'd gotten used to dumping on Dad, and she couldn't bring herself to do that with a therapist *about* Dad.

She jammed her hands into her hair and tried to shake the thoughts from her head.

"You have a headache, Drew?"

She spun around at the sound of Rob's voice. How had he managed to sneak up on her like that? "No, just fixing my hair."

"Oh. Gotcha." In other words, Rob knew she was lying. What a doorknob she must look like to him.

"I just saw Claire," he said. "She said you were looking for me?"

Thanks, Claire. "I was, but no biggie. I'm late for work. I'll catch you later, if that's all right."

"Sure. I'll swing by after I finish my shift."

He turned and walked back down the hall in the direction he'd come, then cut through a side door that led outside.

He was entirely too good-looking for his own good. Or for hers.

Exactly seven hours and fifty-three minutes later, Drew untied the apron she wore while working in the kitchen and hung it on its hook. She grabbed a bag of trash, told one of the kitchen guys she was going to take it to the Dumpster, then signed out. It was a few minutes early, but she wasn't up for seeing Rob. What could she say to him?

And even if she had thought of what to say, she didn't want to say it while she smelled like dishwashing detergent. She walked around the outside of the kitchen, tossed the bag through the Dumpster door, then headed for her cabin. Her ankle felt a lot better than it had yesterday. She tested it by jogging a few steps and cringed. Nope. Not ready for prime time yet.

Maybe she could change into her running clothes and go to the gym, get in a good weight workout. In another few days she could try some light cardio work. Hopefully she wouldn't lose much speed with her downtime.

"Hey, you."

She looked up to see Rob sitting on her front porch. His face was pink, as if he'd forgotten to use enough sunscreen, but otherwise he looked like the same fabulous Rob he always did. And just like it had the first day she'd met him, her mouth actually watered.

How did he *do* that?

"Hey, you, right back," she managed.

"I got finished with my last group a few minutes ago and figured I'd wait here for you. Maybe catch you before Seneca and Claire got back to the cabin," he said.

"Are they here?"

"Nope."

Probably best. They'd be peeking out the windows and making faces at her, or saying things like "We should leave you two alone" while they made a show of going up to the lodge.

She sat down on the porch next to him. Before she could say anything Rob said, "When Claire said you were looking for me this morning, that wasn't really true, was it? It was something she made up to get me to talk to you."

Drew couldn't help but laugh. "She's pretty transparent, huh?"

"No."

When Drew glanced sideways at him, he said, "But you were. When I caught you in the hall, you looked almost as panicked as you did with that bear. Like I was the last person you wanted to see."

"So I'm the one who's transparent."

He slid closer to her. "Not usually."

What was it Cory said? When you're feeling stressed out or overwhelmed, to mentally take yourself to mountain pose. Drew took a deep breath, just like Cory had shown them at the beginning of class, then said, "Look, Rob. I'm sorry I've been avoiding you. It's just, well, I'm sorry I lost it the other day." She fumbled for the right words. "I'm really embarrassed. I'm not the type to spew my problems on other people. Let alone just *spew*."

Rob laughed, then leaned back just enough to put one arm behind her. He didn't touch her, but he didn't give her much room to move, either. "Look, Drew, I like you.

I like you a lot. You're fun to run with, you enjoy hiking and the mountains as much as I do, and you're probably the most beautiful girl I've ever met."

Drew snorted. "What kind of drugs are running through your bloodstream today? You've met my roommate Seneca, haven't you? The girl looks like she should be in the ads in one of Claire's magazines."

Rob didn't laugh at her words this time. "She's pretty, but she's not my type. You don't need makeup or anything to be beautiful. And I think you're as beautiful inside as out."

Oh, no. He was churning out major cheese here.

"But," he continued, "all that sappy stuff aside, what I was going to say is that you don't have to apologize to me. You've been going through something really serious—probably the most serious thing you'll face in your entire life—losing one parent and feeling like you're starting to lose the other, in a way. I don't think most people could hold it together the way you have. So don't be embarrassed. I *admire* you for that."

He did?

"My best friend was killed in a car crash last year," Rob said, his tone surprisingly matter-of-fact. "I was a mess for weeks afterward. I didn't go to school, even when my parents tried to force me. I just hung out in my room and stared at the walls and kept asking God why. I got mad at my friend for driving while he was talking on his cell. I got mad at myself for not being there to stop him from plowing into a ditch at forty miles an hour." Rob let out a long breath. "The thing is, I'm not over it. I don't know if I ever will be. But I *do* understand what you're going through. And believe me, you're handling it a lot better than I did."

Drew shook her head in disbelief. "You must've been *really* screwed up, 'cause I'm not handling it well." At least she hadn't in front of Rob.

"I was. It just took time. And with everything that's going on with your mom, and the fact that this is your parents, not a buddy . . . well, parents are different. It's going to take you some time."

He shifted so he could see if anyone came down the path, but stayed close to her. Still not touching, but close. "I'm your friend, Drew. I'm more if you want me to be more—I think we both know we've been attracted to each other from the instant we met—but if not, and we just stay friends and running partners, that's cool by me, too. No pressure whatsoever."

Damn. He was making her sniffly. She looked up at the porch ceiling and blinked to clear her eyes. *Control.* She needed to stay in control.

"The thing is, Rob, I like you, too. A lot. And I like that you're my friend. I haven't had a close friend in a long, long time—though I'm getting to be friends with Claire and even with Seneca. But I don't think I can handle having a boyfriend. Not until I sort out everything that's happened with my parents."

Even as she said the words, she knew she didn't mean it. She wanted a boyfriend—bad—she just didn't want to lose control of her life, to stop doing things the way *she* wanted to do them. And having a boyfriend meant losing control, if her mom or even the girls at school were anything to judge by.

"I'm going to play armchair psychiatrist for a sec," he said. "You can take or leave my advice, all right?"

"Fine." Here it came. The typical "You'd be happier with me" crap that all guys said in order to get a girl to trust them.

"Did you run as hard as you do now before your dad was killed?"

She hadn't been expecting that. "What?"

"You don't have to answer the question. At least, you don't have to tell me the answer. But think about it. I've wondered if you run as hard as you do because either you need the escape—and if that's true, well, it sure beats having drugs in your bloodstream—or if you're doing it to give yourself a sense of permanence. If your name is up on a wall somewhere, or listed on a website as the record holder in the 2,000 meters or as a winner at a cross-country meet, it'll make you feel immortal. Like you can live forever. Maybe because you've had it shoved in your face in the most awful way possible that we *don't* live forever."

Drew looked down at her shoes, then picked a piece of grass out of the laces. "Boy, when you said armchair psychiatry, you weren't kidding. And nice job working that drugs-in-the-bloodstream comment back in. That was very well done."

"Thanks." He laughed. "But like I said, you don't have to tell me jack. I just want you to think about it."

She nodded and picked another piece of grass from her shoelaces. After a few heartbeats she turned and looked at him. He seemed relaxed, like they weren't talking about anything heavy. She couldn't help but smile at him. "So, how'd you leap from the maybe-we-can-be-more-than-friends to that?"

He shrugged. "You said you weren't sure you were ready for a boyfriend yet because of what happened with your parents. It occurred to me as you said it that something you thought was permanent—having your parents around and stable—wasn't. And somewhere in here"—he tapped his chest—"you believe that if you get a boyfriend and break up, you'll get that same feeling, like something you hoped was permanent wasn't after all, and that you'll get hurt. And the last thing you need in your life right now is to get hurt."

Drew raised an eyebrow. "What are you saying? That you want to go out, or that you want to break up?"

He grabbed the grass from her fingers and tossed it to the side. "I'm saying that I'm very happy just being *friends*. And I mean that. It's not a line. But"—he scooted so he could look at her straight on—"I'm also saying that if we *did* decide to be more than friends, we can take it slow. I can't guarantee neither of us would ever get hurt, but I think if we're careful, we could be adult enough about it not to hurt each other intentionally. And I think we're both strong enough to deal—even if you don't think you are right now—because *if* we did go out, and *if* we eventually broke up, we'd know it was for the best."

Drew leaned back so her head was against one of the posts supporting the porch roof. Maybe he was right. She couldn't help wanting him, but she didn't want to end up spending weeks moping like Claire if it didn't work out.

Then again, even Claire admitted that her breakup with Aaron was for the best. That she was doing the right thing by not trying to get him back.

"This is a crazy conversation," she finally said. "Who plans a breakup before they even decide if they should go out?"

"People who care about their friendship." He stretched his feet out so he could capture one of hers between his, just like he'd done in the cafeteria.

Neither one of them spoke, but Drew realized as she looked at Rob, and as she felt his hiking boots hooked onto either side of her running shoe, that he might be worth the risk. And maybe she was stronger than she thought.

"I'll tell you what," she said. "Forget the armchair psychiatry and let's go for a walk. I want to test my ankle out. And maybe, *maybe*, if you can prove to me that you can keep from analyzing me like some nutcase, I'll even hold your hand."

His mouth cinched up on one side in a way that made Drew's stomach knot. Did he have any clue how good-looking he was? "I have no desire to be your therapist, Drew, so I think you're safe."

"Good. I have no desire to be your therapist, either."

He let go of her feet, then stood. When she was standing, too, he reached his right hand toward her. "Shake on it?"

She grinned, then slipped her hand into his. It felt

even better than that first, awkward handshake they'd shared when she'd introduced herself, when she realized he wouldn't break her hand to prove how strong he was or treat her like she was a first-class dork from Kansas.

She'd figured right then that he'd treat her like an equal. It was the way he was built, the way he viewed the world. And he still looked at her that way, even though she'd cried in front of him. Puked in front of him. Let him see how scared out of her wits she could get.

Nothing about him had changed; he still respected her, same as on that first day, when he'd talked to her about working as a trail guide.

But he had certainly changed her. And for the better.

"Oh, what the hell." Instead of letting go of his hand she pulled him forward and stretched up onto her tiptoes. "Let's try this out."

She kissed him.

And he kissed her right back.

✲✲✲ TWENTY-ONE ✲✲✲

Claire undid the rubber band from a stack of brochures on whitewater rafting, then stuck them in the appropriate place on the large rack of tourist info beside the information desk. A few brochures for other destinations—a couple of local restaurants, an old cog-train ride, Rocky Mountain National Park— were jammed in odd spots, so she pulled them out, smoothed them, and put them in their proper places.

Perfect. All neat and orderly.

She heard someone approaching and turned, ready to give out whatever information the guest might need.

The face smiling at her didn't belong to a guest. "Hi, Todd! Whatcha doing here?"

"Bringing you our new brochures. Dad is having me drive around town and restock." He dropped the pile of red brochures he'd been holding onto her desk, then picked one off the top and flipped it open.

"Check it out. New trail map and everything."

Claire grinned. "Yeah, I seem to recall that during his discussion of forest preservation your dad mentioned that he was closing one of the older trails and opening a new one with . . . what was his phrase?"

"'Less environmental impact,'" Todd finished. "I can't believe you were so desperate to avoid me you listened to him for so long."

"Me, either."

Todd looked around the lobby, observing the family getting ready to walk through the rear doors and join their hiking guide, and the group of women gathering at the front door to go on a shopping outing to Juniper's boutiques. "Well, looks like you're having a blast here."

"It's not that bad. I like it." She tried not to sound too corny as she added, "And it's good to see you here."

"Thanks. It's good not to be intentionally avoided." He said it in a tone that let her know he forgave her, which made her feel better.

"So, before I go dump another stack of these at every hotel in town, what are you up to tonight? There's a band playing at The Final Run that everyone's been buzzing about, but I really want to skip the scene. I . . . I've been doing some thinking lately, and I'm just not sure I want to do that anymore. At all. Even without alcohol, it's too much."

"Oh." It was all Claire could manage.

"I thought maybe I could talk you into coming over to my parents' place and watching a movie down in the theater room," he continued. "You can invite your roommates if you want. We'll make popcorn, drink some Coke—without any rum or Jack Daniels in it—and just have a laid-back, fun evening."

It sounded so fun. But she just couldn't. Before she could say anything Todd said, "No big deal. We can do it another night."

"No, I really want to do it," Claire explained. "But—and don't make fun of me—I wanted to go to Teen Jam tonight. I haven't been since school got out, and I really want to go."

Todd looked surprised. "You're really serious about it, huh?"

She nodded. "You were right about Aaron the other day. I mean, about spring break waking me up. It's more complicated than that, but—"

"Going to Teen Jam is helping you figure things out."

"Exactly." If Delia and Amanda would quit giving her such nasty looks, it'd be easier, but she couldn't stop trying. She got so much out of the meeting last time, listening to the minister talk about making good decisions, that she knew it'd be worth facing them to go again.

And she had a goal, too, now that she'd committed to Mexico.

"Then let's plan on movies another night. You name the day, and I'm there."

"Sounds great. Thanks."

Todd grinned, then turned to go. He'd only taken a few steps when Claire sensed she was being watched. She spun around and, sure enough, Amanda was standing in the door to the dining room, wearing her King's Crown polo and holding a tray of empty glassware.

She couldn't possibly have heard what she and Todd were talking about, but she was glaring as if Claire had called her a dirty name.

Amanda set the tray down on a rack near the door, glanced over her shoulder, then strode out of the dining room and across the lobby. "I knew it," she hissed. "You had no interest in coming to Teen Jam and making friends. All that stuff you said about meeting new people? Yeah, total lie if you're still hanging with Mirelli and his crowd. You can't have it both ways, Claire."

"Hey, what time were you planning to leave for Teen Jam?" Todd's voice came from behind her, surprising Claire.

She spun around. "Um, it starts at seven, so six thirty?"

"Think you can leave by quarter after and give me a ride? That way, you can introduce me around." He closed the gap between them, then looked from Claire to Amanda. "Hey, Amanda. How's it going? Did Claire tell you she's bringing me to Teen Jam tonight? You go, don't you?"

The stunned expression on Amanda's face was price-less. "Yeah. I go."

"Well, guess I'll see you there." He paused, then shot a pointed look behind her. "Um, I think your boss is looking for you."

Claire looked past Amanda. "Oh, no. Marla patrol. You'd better get in there." She gave Amanda a huge smile and added, "See you tonight, though!"

"You are soooo bad," she whispered to Todd once Amanda had returned to the dining room, grabbed her tray, and headed toward the kitchen with Marla close behind. "I can't believe you did that. Thanks for the save."

"Anytime." He leaned closer, then said, "So now we're obligated. Pick me up and let me see what this Teen Jam thing is all about."

He was serious? "Are you sure?"

"What are friends for? No promises that I'll go again,

but I can handle it for one night. And it's not like I had other plans."

Claire couldn't help the grin that spread across her face. How could things in her life be going so well? She was getting along with Seneca and Drew, *they* were getting along great with Jake and Rob—as they'd each described in great detail until nearly three a.m.—and now Todd was willing to go with her to Teen Jam? "If I leave here by six fifteen, I can be in your driveway by six thirty."

It'd be fabulous to have a friend at her side when she walked back in to Teen Jam.

And she had a sneaky feeling he would come to like it as much as she did.

✳✳✳ EPILOGUE ✳✳✳

"Hey, I saw on the schedule that Cory's teaching Goddess Yoga again tonight. You guys up for it?" Claire asked as she walked into the cabin at the end of her shift and greeted Seneca and Drew. "Unless you have plans with Jake," she said to Seneca.

"I don't," Seneca said. "But Drew might have plans with Rob, now that her ankle's better. The doctor told her she could try running on it again if she wanted."

"No plans with Rob tonight," Drew said. But the grin on her face made it obvious to Claire that things were still going well between the two of them and that they'd have plans on other nights, even if they didn't tonight. "Goddess Yoga would be fun. I can try the poses without the modifications. Might be a good test before I go full bore and tackle a trail."

"Well, it starts in fifteen minutes," Claire said. "I'm going to grab my stuff."

She went upstairs to pack a gym bag, and both Seneca and Drew followed.

"Wonder what kind of goddess story Cory will tell tonight?" Drew asked.

"I dunno," Seneca said. "I asked her today at the spa, but she wouldn't even give me a hint. I noticed there was a new book on mythology in the waiting area, though. Jake and I read a little bit of it at lunch. Did you guys know that goddesses hardly ever got along with one another? The Three Fates were, like, a total exception to the rule. They were some of the only goddesses who worked together."

Drew looped her gym bag over her shoulder, then grabbed her water bottle as Seneca and Claire did the same. No one moved for the stairs. They all just looked at one another with silly grins on their faces.

"So, are we regular goddesses? Or the Three Goddesses?" Claire asked.

"The Three Goddesses!" Drew and Seneca both shouted, and they all collapsed in a fit of laughter.

"Later tonight, when we're done, let's come back here," Drew said. "There's stuff I've been meaning to tell you guys for a long time."

"Me too," Claire said.

"Sounds serious," Seneca said, her voice full of worry.

"It's serious, but something I need to get off my chest," Drew said. "What about you, Claire?"

"Same thing. It's just—" She shrugged. "I guess I didn't trust you guys before. But I do now. And I think I'd feel better talking to you both."

She needed to tell someone what happened with Aaron. Just to purge it all from her system. They didn't need to know *everything*, but maybe it'd help them to understand why Teen Jam was becoming so important to her. Why she needed to have time to read her Bible in the morning and to meditate about what God wanted for her.

"Well, I don't have anything heavy to share," Seneca said. "But I want to hear what both of you have to say. And then . . ." She waited a moment, all drama as usual, then said, "When you guys are done with your serious stuff, I'll tell you all some good news. My mom got a new agent today. She called me at work and gave me all the details. Someone from CAA called and courted her, so she switched. She feels really good about it, like it's going to be a whole new start for her career."

Claire and Drew started to ask questions, but Seneca waved them off. "Nope, nope, I'm not going to say any more. Yoga first. Then Drew, you talk. Then you, Claire. For once I'm going to put you guys first. But we need to hustle or we're going to be late for class."

Claire raised her water bottle. "This is going to be totally dorky on my part, but before we go I want to make a toast. To the Three Goddesses. Lifelong friends. May we all grow to be as close as the Three Fates were."

"What was it Cory said about them at that first class?" Seneca asked. "That they were inextricably tied together, right?"

"Yep," Claire said. "So . . . to the Three Goddesses!"

Drew and Seneca raised their bottles and tapped them against Claire's.

"And *namaste*." Drew added. "All that is good in my soul recognizes and honors all that is good in yours."

"*Namaste*," Seneca and Claire repeated.

As the cool water hit her throat, Claire decided it was the best drink she'd had in years.